Gwyneth Rees is half Welsh and half English and grew up in Scotland. She went to Glasgow University and qualified as a doctor in 1990. She is a child and adolescent psychiatrist and has worked in several places, including Birmingham and London. She is the author of *Mermaid Magic*, *Fairy Dust*, *Fairy Treasure*, *Cosmo and the Magic Sneeze* and, for older readers, *The Mum Hunt*, winner of the Award for Younger Children in the Red House Children's Book Award 2004. She lives in London with her two cats.

Visit www.gwynethrees.com

Other books by Gwyneth Rees

Mermaid Magic
Fairy Dust
Fairy Treasure
Cosmo and the Magic Sneeze

For older readers

The Mum Hunt

Look out for

The Mum Detective
Fairy Dreams

My Mum's from Planet Pluto

Gwyneth Rees

MACMILLAN CHILDREN'S BOOKS

To Eve D'Souza

First published 2004 by Macmillan Children's Books

This edition published 2005 by Macmillan Children's Books
a division of Macmillan Publishers Ltd
20 New Wharf Road, London N1 9RR
Basingstoke and Oxford
www.panmacmillan.com

Associated companies throughout the world

ISBN 0 330 43728 3

1 3 5 7 9 8 6 4 2

A CIP catalogue record for this book is available from
the British Library.

Typeset by Intype Libra Ltd
Printed and bound in Great Britain by Mackays of Chatham plc, Kent

1

'Daniel, I don't see how you can write an essay when you're not even concentrating on it,' Mum said crossly.

It was three weeks after we'd moved house and I was perched on the settee with my feet on the coffee table, trying to watch *Neighbours* and do my summer project. I'd been getting along quite well until Mum came into the room. Mum has this annoying habit of planting herself between me and the television set whenever I'm trying to watch TV and do my homework at the same time. I'm perfectly capable of doing both, but Mum refuses to believe that.

My mum, who's called Isabel, is a teacher and you might think that since she spends all day at work lecturing children she'd want to give it a rest when she comes home, but you'd be wrong. Mum never bats an eyelid if I moan at her for being all teachery at home. She just replies that she likes to get in as much *practice* as possible (especially in the summer holidays, when she might get out of the habit), so isn't it lucky that she's got me?

She said something else which I didn't hear because I was too caught up in listening to *Neighbours*. Some psychotic madman had taken everybody hostage in the coffee shop three episodes ago. He said he'd planted a bomb in there and he was going to set it off if the police didn't meet his demands. Now the police were saying it was just a hoax and they were about to storm the building. The thing was, in the previous episode they'd actually shown this bomb, ticking away under one of the tables, so you knew that it wasn't really a hoax. Any minute now the bomb was going to go off and there were going to be cappuccinos and blown-up bodies flying about all over the place. I leaned sideways in an attempt to see past Mum.

'You didn't hear a word of what I just said, did you?' Mum accused me, shifting her position in order to block the TV more effectively. She had raised her voice so I couldn't hear what the coffee-shop hijacker was saying to the pregnant lady who was screaming because she was about to give birth to twins and he still wouldn't let her out of the shop.

'Shush, Mum . . .' I looked up at her in alarm, realizing my mistake immediately.

'I beg your pardon?' Her brow had furrowed and her eyes were glinty. 'You watch far too much television, Daniel!' She reached behind her and switched it off.

'*Mum!*' I yelled.

'I was *saying*,' she continued doggedly, 'that the *beginning* of any piece of writing has to grab the attention if you want your reader to carry on reading it.'

'Mrs Lyle has *got* to carry on reading it,' I pointed out, staring crossly at the blank TV screen. 'It's her job!'

Mum winced, as if I had just reminded her of a very painful fact. That didn't shut her up though. Sighing a sigh of great sympathy for Mrs Lyle, my new head of year, and all other teachers including herself, she continued, 'And that is precisely why you should try to hand in something that is not *too* unbearable to read. A little effort is what's required, Daniel. A little concentration.' She was looking at me as though she thought I was a lost cause. 'Honestly, I know your father doesn't think you've got that attention deficit disorder or whatever it's called, but I'm really not so sure!'

That made me see red. My concentration – or lack of it – is something Mum's been harping on about forever and even Dad gets cross with her sometimes because he says her expectations are too high. He told her that when he thought I wasn't listening one time. (He'd never say that if he thought I *was* listening because he believes that parents should always present a united front – even if they're both wrong.)

'There's nothing wrong with *my* head . . .' I said sharply.

Mum gave me a surprised – and hurt – look and I instantly felt guilty. We don't normally talk about the times when Mum's been ill. The last time she'd had to be admitted to a psychiatric hospital was seven years ago when my sister, Martha, was born.

I tried to make myself feel better by telling myself I didn't care if I hurt Mum's feelings. After all, she shouldn't say horrible things about me if she doesn't want me to say stuff back.

3

'All I'm trying to do is encourage you, Daniel,' Mum said, softly now. 'But if you don't care what Mrs Lyle thinks of your work, then that's your lookout.' And she left the room.

'I *don't* care what Mrs Lyle thinks!' I called out after her, because now that she'd reminded me about my new school, I could get angry with her again. After all, it was her fault we'd had to move here.

I looked down at the empty page of my new jotter. I *would* have minded what my class teacher at my *old* school thought because I liked her and I liked my old school. But Mrs Lyle was just a name to me because term hadn't even started back yet and, in any case, I thought it was really dumb of her to send out letters to all the Year Sevens who were going to be starting secondary school for the first time in September, asking them to prepare an introductory essay about themselves over the summer. Even Dad had commented that he thought it was a bit zealous of her, although he'd supported Mum in insisting I do it just the same.

I turned the TV back on and threw my homework jotter on the floor.

Before we'd moved, Mum had been Deputy Head at a secondary school on the other side of the city from where we lived. She had gone for several interviews over the last year and when she finally got offered her very first head teacher's job, I was busy congratulating her like everybody else until I asked whereabouts in the city her new school actually was, and she told me it was on the south coast. The thing was, that was miles away. We'd driven to

4

the south coast one summer for a holiday and it had taken us a whole day to get there.

The really annoying thing was that nobody else in my family seemed to mind as much as me. My dad, who's called Malcolm, said he'd always secretly fancied living by the sea. He's a GP and he joked that there'd be plenty of work for him since seaside towns are full of doddery old people who have to go and see their doctors a lot. My little sister, Martha, liked the idea of living near the beach too. I was the one who hated the idea of leaving our old place the most – and *then* I found out that in our new town I'd be expected to go to the same school as Mum. I begged and begged to be allowed to go to a different school, even if it meant travelling on six different buses every morning to get there. Mum and Dad did give it some thought, but in the end they said that the school where Mum would be working was far and away the best school in the area and that they didn't feel they should make any sacrifices where my education was concerned. Dad was sympathetic but said he was sure that I had what it took to cope and Mum promised that she'd try to be as little of an embarrassment to me as possible (which, when you consider what happened later, turned out to be the biggest joke ever).

I couldn't get back into *Neighbours* properly after that, so when Mum came back into the room, I looked up from the TV immediately.

She didn't say anything about the television being back on. 'Come on. It's about time we took those membership forms back to the library. There might be time for you to choose a book today. We can pick Martha up from her singing class on the way back.'

Martha, my little sister, is seven-and-a-half (she'd want you to remember the half) and she's the sort of little girl that aunties and grannies and other people's mothers all say they want to take home and keep. I've got to admit that she does look really cute. She doesn't look like Mum or Dad or me because we're all dark and she's got fair hair. It's bobbed at her shoulders and she's got these big blue eyes and pink cheeks with dimples. She's always playing some daft pretend game or other and trying to get me to join in. That's unless she's got her new friend Sally with her, in which case she screams at me to go away if I try and set foot in her room. The summer singing class had been Mum's idea. When Martha had protested that she *couldn't* sing, Mum had said that that was an excellent reason then for joining a singing class, wasn't it? I knew the real reason Mum wanted us to join things was so we'd make friends quickly. She'd tried to get me to join some things too, but so far I'd resisted.

As we drove to the library, I stared grumpily out of the car window. I was thinking about how I didn't know a single other person who lived here and how all I wanted was to start at the secondary school in our old town with my old friends. My best friend, Mark, was going there and since our surnames both start with the letter M – mine is MacKenzie and his is Morrison – we thought we might get put in the same classes for stuff, though I wasn't sure if that was how they sorted things out in secondary school. Still, if they did it on academic ability, Mark and I should still have been in the same classes. Except for Maths. Mark's a lot better than me at Maths. And I'm better at creative writing. At least, I am when I'm in the right mood.

'I only wanted to see what happened,' I complained crossly to my mother.

'Sorry?' Mum was concentrating on fiddling with the radio, which was making a horrible crackling noise.

'In *Neighbours*. I only wanted to see who got blown up.'

'Oh, you and your television, Daniel,' Mum said, frowning as a plop of seagull pooh landed on the windscreen. 'It's not good for you. In fact, we should probably get rid of the TV set completely. Maybe that way we'd get you to read some books.'

'NO!' I protested. I know it sounds crazy but the TV seemed to have become really important to me ever since we'd moved. It was very comforting, somehow, to watch the same characters and same stories carrying on as normal when everything in *my* life had completely changed. I sometimes wished I could jump inside the television set and stay there. Or that I could just switch off my real life whenever I got fed up with it, the same way you can switch off a TV programme you don't like.

Mum was looking for a place to park outside the library.

'You can never find anywhere in this street. Get your head out of the way please, Daniel. I can't see.' She said a rude word as another car beat her to the parking space she'd just spotted. 'Listen, why don't I just let you out of the car here and you can hand in the forms and choose a book while I go and pick up Martha? I'll meet you here again in twenty minutes. OK?'

'Mum—' I wanted to ask her again about the television, to make sure she wasn't really considering getting rid of it.

'And make sure you pick a book that you're actually going to read.'

I knew it was no use pursuing the subject of television when Mum's mind was on books. I got out of the car, slamming the door a lot harder than I needed to.

Sometimes Mum really makes me mad. I know she only wants what she thinks is best for me, but the trouble is that what *she* thinks is best isn't always what *I* think is best. Dad's no help because he agrees with her most of the time – just for a quiet life, I reckon. He even lets her tell him what she thinks is best for *him*, though a lot of the time he just goes and does the opposite when she's not looking.

Well, Mum isn't always right, at least not about me. For one thing, she thinks I hate going to the library, but actually I like it.

The library is probably about the only place in our new town that I think is an improvement on our old one. The library where we used to live was a large, airy, modern building on one level with lots of skylight windows. When it was raining, the rain used to make a terrific clattering noise on those windows. The library here is an old building – Mum says it's at least a hundred years old – that must have once been a very grand private house. I like to imagine it how it used to be, with the big reception area as the

8

main entrance hall, with a maid coming to take your coat and a butler appearing to announce you. There's a wide, twisting, marble staircase that leads up to the reference section, and I could almost see all the ladies sweeping down it in their big, fancy ballgowns, and hear the music as everyone waltzed around the room in the adult reading section or sipped champagne served from silver trays in the children's corner.

That afternoon was the second time I'd been there. The first time we'd popped in quickly to collect the membership forms. There was nobody at the reception desk when I walked in now. Maybe they were busy putting books away or something. I put the completed forms on the desk and went to have a look in the junior readers' section.

I found a book and took it over to the children's corner where there were some little kids' seats. I sat down, opened the book at the first page and started to read. I always try to read at least the first page, and if possible the whole first chapter, of any book to make sure I really like it before I take it out of the library, because last time I got bored with a book halfway through and gave up reading it, Mum seized upon the fact like it was a major piece of evidence in a courtroom trial: 'This just proves what I've been saying all along! You're losing the art of reading! It's all that passive entertainment you get from sitting in front of the television, that's what it is! It's making your brain lazy!' And she wouldn't let me watch any more TV until I'd finished the book and told her the entire plot.

But I don't mind reading if it's a good book.

Good books are just as easy to escape into as television – better in our house, because my mum doesn't keep interrupting all the time. I was just starting to get interested in this one when the library door banged shut and loud footsteps sounded on the wooden floor.

A female voice boomed out, sounding slurred. 'Getchyourself a book then, Abby. Hurry up.' I was still getting used to the way people speak here. They have funny voices which Dad says are on account of the flat vowel sounds they have instead of the nicer bouncier ones we use in the north. Though Dad suggested I shouldn't actually point that out to anyone when I started at my new school. As if I'd be that stupid.

'It's OK, Mum. I just need to hand these in.' A girl about my age came into view. She had straight, shoulder-length, light-brown hair and a suntanned face. She was wearing a long brown cotton skirt, a red top and black trainers with red laces. She clutched two books against her chest as she glanced around for the librarian, who still wasn't behind her desk.

The girl's mother pushed past her. She had a puffy red face and short untidy hair. She started to walk clumsily towards the children's section, where I was sitting. 'Look at these liddle plashtic seats – you have to have a liddle bottom to sit on them!' She laughed loudly. Her breath, now that she was close to me, smelt like my Uncle Robert's does when he's had too much beer at Christmas.

I jumped up and my chair fell over. I felt myself flush.

The woman laughed as I bent down to pick it up. The girl called Abby came over to her then and grabbed her arm. Her face was bright red too – with embarrassment at having a mum like that, I reckoned – and she avoided looking at me. 'C'mon, Mum. We have to get back.'

But the woman had already plonked herself down on the rug where some toddlers' books had been left out. 'Look at this!' she said, lifting one up, dangling it by a corner for a moment, then dropping it noisily on to the floor.

The girl saw me staring at her mother and glared at me. 'What are *you* looking at?'

'Nothing,' I said, quickly moving to leave. I hurried over to the bookshelves and put my book back.

Mum was waiting outside for me in the car and Martha was waving to me from the back seat. I waved back. I might moan about my little sister, but she thinks I'm great and that makes her pretty nice to be around most of the time.

Now, as I climbed into the car, I glanced back at the library steps and saw the girl called Abby and her mother come out. I wondered if Abby had a dad. I hoped so, because maybe her dad could help her with her mum.

I looked across at *my* mum, suddenly feeling much less angry with her. Mum always *looks* good no matter what. She's got these dark-blue eyes that Dad says come from her Irish ancestors and lots of thick dark hair which she only ties back when she's at work. People sometimes turn to have a second look at her in the street, though she doesn't seem to notice that. All Mum notices about herself is that she's plumper than she wants to be, which she's always blaming on the lithium. That's the name of the medication she has to take every day to stop getting ill again like she was before. The lithium keeps the chemicals in her brain from getting unbalanced. We've all got chemicals in our brain but some people's work better than other people's. That's how Mum explained it to me one time. You'd think Dad would explain it since he's the doctor in our family, not her, but Dad never likes me asking questions about Mum's illness. Anyway, the lithium tablets Mum takes keep her brain chemicals working the same as everybody else's, but one of the side effects of the medication is that it makes her put on weight more easily. Mum hates that. I've told her lots of times that she's not *horrendously* fat, but she just says, 'Gee, thanks, Daniel,' and carries on glaring at herself in the mirror.

'Mum, I'm sorry about before,' I said now, as I fastened my seatbelt.

'I'm sorry too,' Mum said. 'Now . . . is this coming-out-of-the-library-with-no-book an act of rebellion, or could you just not find a good one?'

I grinned and said that there just hadn't been any good ones and she said, 'What? In the whole library?' But I could tell she wasn't really angry with me.

Then we both listened while Martha told us how one of the boys had made a bad smell in her singing class and everyone had had to hold their noses while they were singing.

By the time we got home, I was feeling much

more chilled about everything and I cheered up even more when I saw that Dad's car was back in the driveway. He had been to visit a couple of GP practices that afternoon to see about applying for a new job.

The chilled feeling didn't last though. It was while Martha and I were in the kitchen raiding the cupboard for crisps that Mum and Dad asked us to sit down because they had something important to tell us.

'Good or bad?' I asked, swinging my kitchen chair back on two legs and banging it down again.

'Just sit still and *listen* for a minute, will you, Daniel . . .' Dad said, sounding impatient, which made me stop fidgeting straight away, because Dad hardly ever sounds like that.

And that's when he told us that he was going to New Zealand for two months – and that he was leaving a week on Saturday.

2

'Daniel, you've been on that phone long enough!'

It was the following morning and Dad was running a bath for Martha. Mum had gone up to the hospital for an outpatient appointment. This was her first appointment since we'd moved and the reason it had come so promptly was because Dad had phoned up and spoken to the psychiatrist himself.

I ignored Dad and carried on talking to my friend Mark from back home. If I was still living at our old place, I'd be down at the park playing football with him right now. We played football nearly every day last summer holidays. I was telling Mark what Dad had told us yesterday – that he had decided to postpone starting a new job here in order to go to New Zealand to visit his mother one last time. Our grandmother, who I'd only ever met three times because she emigrated with my aunt the year before I was born, was diagnosed with cancer last year. We'd already been on this big family holiday to New Zealand last summer to see her, and she'd looked perfectly OK to me. I hadn't expected her to look OK. I thought it was scary because it meant that lots of other people who looked OK could really have a cancer growing inside them. I kept asking Dad how I could tell if *I* had one and in the end he got really upset and shouted at me.

Mum had come to talk to me afterwards. (Usually it's the other way round – Mum shouts at me and Dad's the one who comes to talk to me later.) Mum said he'd shouted because he was only just managing to bear the fact that his mother was dying and that right now he didn't have any strength left to imagine me – his child – as anything but immortal.

That set me off thinking, I remember. I thought about how when Dad and I had watched the DVD of *Highlander* together – where the guy is immortal and can't ever die – Dad had said that being immortal would be the worst thing ever. He'd said he couldn't imagine anything more awful than having to watch everyone you loved grow old and die while never getting to rest in peace yourself. So I seriously doubted that Dad would really want me to be immortal.

But before I could say any of this, Mum had added, 'Daniel, your father is hurting really badly inside right now. So don't just blurt things out like you usually do. *Think* first. Please.'

So I did think and I did my best to be really nice to Dad the whole of the rest of the time we were in New Zealand. I made him drinks with all different types of fruit juice in them and called them funny names like Bloody Malcolm (that was orange juice mixed with tomato juice) and Bogeyman Surprise (that was a green one with kiwis and bananas in it). And I made a special effort to be extra polite to my gran, even though I've always found her a bit strict and scary. I even pretended not to mind the fact that she said Martha could have her china doll when she died, whereas I wasn't getting anything.

Anyway, the doctors didn't think my gran would last this long, but since she had – and it was going to be her seventy-fifth birthday at the end of September – Dad had decided he wanted to go and see her again. He'd talked it over with Mum, who was really supportive of him going. Mum's an only child and so were both her parents, so she didn't have any family left after they died when she was in her twenties and she's always saying how she wishes she'd spent more time with them.

Dad had booked his flight for the Saturday after we started at our new schools.

'It's a bummer you can't go with him,' Mark said when I told him all this on the phone.

'I know,' I agreed.

'I've got to go now,' Mark added. 'I promised I'd be at Billy's house by half-ten . . .' He sounded a bit awkward again, like he had at the beginning of our conversation. It had been fine once we'd got going, but somehow it had seemed to take us both a little while to start chatting as easily to each other as we always used to. I don't know why. Mark had even said, 'How are you?' when he first came to the phone, really politely, like I was a complete stranger. I mean, we absolutely never asked each other how we were – not unless one of us was off sick with chickenpox or something. And now he was in a rush to meet Billy, who Mark had always said got on his nerves before when he tried to hang out with the two of us.

'DANIEL!' Dad shouted down the stairs.

'See you, Mark,' I said, slamming down the phone and instantly blaming my dad for our conversation having to end before I was ready. Feeling angry with Mark wasn't an option. I missed him too much.

'I thought it was just teenage girls who spent ages on the telephone,' Dad said lightly. 'And I thought I asked you to wash up the breakfast things *before* you phoned Mark.'

'*Mum* stays on the phone much longer than that!' I snapped.

Dad looked surprised. '*Mum* is one of the people in this house who pays the phone bill. *She* can stay on the phone however long she likes.'

'Fine. *I'll* start paying the phone bill too then. You can take it out of my pocket money – there's nothing else to spend it on here anyway!'

'Daniel . . . stop being silly . . .' Dad came down the stairs towards me. Unlike Mum, he hardly ever loses his temper with me no matter how obnoxious I'm being. He stooped to pick up my trainer, which had been lying on the stairs for the past two days, and handed it to me. 'Come on . . . It'll be easier once school starts back. You'll make some new friends.'

'No I won't,' I snarled. 'Not when everyone finds out my mum is the new head! Anyway, *you* don't like it here either!'

'Huh?' He put his hand out to stop me as I made to push past him up the stairs. 'What do you mean?'

'I heard you on the phone the other night to Uncle Robert. You told him you missed your old job much more than you thought you would and on a rainy day this has to be the dreariest little town you've ever encountered in all your forty-three years!' Uncle Robert is Dad's best friend and he's the nearest thing to a proper uncle we've got. Dad had been on the phone to him the other night for even longer than I'd just been on the phone to Mark.

Dad let go of my arm, looking uncomfortable. He pulled a face, then gave me a weak grin. 'Didn't I say *dearest*, not *dreariest*?'

'No you did not!' I snarled, pushing past him to get upstairs, where I collided with Martha on the landing as she came stumbling out of her bedroom in her pink pyjamas to see what all the noise was about.

'DAD-DY!' She let out a deafening shriek as if I'd just tried to murder her or something.

I glared at her. After all, I hadn't bumped into her on purpose, had I? Then I saw that she was looking past me, into the bathroom. Foamy water was gushing down the side of the bath on to the carpet.

As Dad came thudding up the stairs, I decided this would be a good time to escape. I grabbed my favourite jacket from the floor of my bedroom and paused for a moment to look at myself in the wardrobe mirror as I put it on. I used to have a much chubbier face when I was younger, but I reckon I look much better now that you can see my cheekbones. I've got dark-brown cropped hair that I never think needs combing (though Mum always makes me anyway) and blue eyes like Mum's. I reckoned I looked cool enough to go out and about on my own in my new neighbourhood. Normally I'd have asked

Dad before I took off anywhere but right then I felt like it was my decision, not his.

In the bathroom, Dad and Martha had turned off the taps and were attempting to mop up the flood with a whole heap of towels. They didn't notice me as I trod lightly across the landing and down the stairs.

At the very bottom, I yelled up at them as loudly as I could, 'I'M GOING OUT! SEE YOU LATER!'

Before Dad had a chance to reply I slammed the door and was gone. And I didn't feel the least bit guilty about leaving the breakfast things for him to do. After all, he wouldn't have to do *any* washing-up for a whole two months when he went off without us to New Zealand, would he?

I thought I might be in trouble when I got back, even though I'd only stayed out for an hour. I'd soon got bored, kicking about the streets on my own and, besides, leaving the house without my mum or dad knowing where I've gone is the one thing that's pretty much guaranteed to get me grounded. The punishment varies with the amount of freaking out they've been doing in my absence, so today, after I'd calmed down, I reckoned it was best to get myself back home before Dad had time to get too imaginative about all the nasty things that might be happening to me.

I needn't have worried though. When I got back, Mum had just got in too and I reckoned they'd probably forgotten all about me because the two of them were in the living room having a heated conversation about something else.

'Yes . . . well, I resent you phoning up and speaking to my psychiatrist behind my back as if I'm some sort of child who can't manage her own life,' Mum was saying angrily. 'I told *him* that too!'

'Well, you're not sleeping that well, Izzy . . . I was worried . . .'

'I told him how you worried about everything. I told him you were more worried before my interview for head than I was! I told him how *you* said you were worried they wouldn't give it to me on account of my health record. Such faith in me you had!'

'Isobel, I *always* had faith in you. I knew you deserved to get it. I was just worried in case they held the medical reports against you, that's all. I know they're not meant to but—'

'What did you worry about after that? I know. You worried about the school governors telling the staff about me. You wanted to phone them up and check they'd keep it confidential. You know health information is always kept confidential, but you still wanted to take over and make a big fuss about it. Well, I'm fed up with you . . . with you *overprotecting* me, Malcolm! I'm fed up with being the one reassuring *you* all the time that there's nothing to worry about!' She paused to take a breath. 'And OK . . . I'm not sleeping well at the moment . . . but there's such a thing as the normal stress of changing jobs and moving house, isn't there?'

'Of course there is,' Dad replied, sounding tired. 'I just wanted to make sure, especially with me going away next week . . .'

I stood still in the hallway, feeling my stomach churn a little bit. I wished Dad wasn't going away.

Martha appeared at the top of the stairs then, holding her teddy in one hand and looking just like Christopher Robin in our Winnie-the-Pooh book, where he's standing on the top stair, dangling Pooh before bumping him all the way downstairs. She looked really little standing there.

I ran upstairs with my arms out in front of me doing my impersonation of Superman, which always makes her giggle. At the top of the stairs I pulled her down on to the floor with me and lay there on my belly with one arm stretched out in front and the other curled round my sister while she giggled and I made whooshing Superman-flying-through-the-air noises.

When I'd stopped my Superman impression I still didn't feel like going back downstairs, so I went into Martha's bedroom and watched her playing for a while. She was making the dolls in her doll's house talk to each other. I think it's really cute the way she does that, so I stayed put and listened to the mummy doll shouting at the daddy doll because he had forgotten to turn off the taps in the bathroom and had flooded the whole house. Which meant that mummy doll then had to call the fire brigade.

'You be the fireman, Daniel,' she ordered me. Then she launched into a high-pitched, posh-mummy voice, holding an imaginary telephone to her ear.

'*This is an emergency. We need you to come and pump all the water out of our house.*'

'*Of course, madam . . . That extra water will come in very handy next time there's a fire . . .*'

We went on like that for a bit until Martha got

fed up with me coming out with smart-alec things in the middle of her story. By the time she chucked me out, I figured it was time to go back downstairs again.

Mum and Dad were in the kitchen now, where Dad was making them both cups of tea.

'Izzy, you *have* to take the dose the doctor prescribes, even if it *is* stopping you from losing weight,' he was saying. 'We can't take any chances, *especially* while I'm away . . .'

'There you go again! You're afraid I can't manage my medication properly without you here to supervise me!' Mum still sounded annoyed.

'Hi,' I said, joining them in the kitchen. 'Um . . . Do you still want me to do the dishes?'

'Daniel . . .' I thought Dad was going to tell me off for not doing the washing-up when I'd first been asked. But instead he said, 'While I'm away I'd like you and Martha to help out more. Especially you. Mum's going to be very busy with her new job and she's going to need you to do your bit.'

'OK, Dad,' I said. 'I'll help out. And don't worry. I'll make sure Mum takes her tablets.'

Mum made a sort of choking noise and nearly spat out her tea, at which point I rushed out of the kitchen to escape the aftermath of the *wrong thing* that I had just blurted out.

Because even though Mum had once been mentally ill, she was not a child and must not be treated like one. And now she was yelling all over again at Dad for putting the ridiculous idea into her twelve-year-old son's head that *he* needed to worry about whether she took her medication or not.

22

3

'Mrs Lyle seems very . . . *pleasant*,' Mum had said when I'd asked her what my new head of year was like. I should have known that meant Mrs Lyle was an old dragon. If Mum likes a person when she first meets them, she calls them something other than *pleasant*. So far she'd called everyone here *really nice* or *so lovely* or *ever so friendly* – except the butcher down the road who didn't sell organic meat. When she'd complained about it he'd told her he didn't intend to order in organic meat just for her and that he could do without her supporting his small local shop, thanks very much, if she was going to be so rude about his perfectly good lamb chops. Dad had got a bit worried when Mum had related that story to him when she got home. He never likes it when Mum gets into arguments with people.

'None of the staff are going to mention to the children about you being related to me,' Mum said the day before school started back.

'Oh, great. Then nobody'll find out. I mean, it's not like we've got the same surname or anything, is it?' I said sarcastically.

'I just meant that none of the staff is going to draw attention to it. Look, Daniel . . .' Mum sighed, sounding a bit impatient. 'With this attitude, you're just going to *make* things turn out badly for yourself.'

'Oh, right! I get it! If I get picked on because you're the head, it'll be all *my* fault!'

'I didn't say that,' Mum replied sharply. 'I just meant that if you keep whining on about—'

'Mum just means that if you let the other children see that you *think* it's a big thing, then they're much more likely to *make* it into a big thing,' Dad interrupted firmly. He does that sometimes – interrupts Mum when she's about to say something, as if he thinks she might not be going to put whatever it is as diplomatically as he could.

I glanced at my father. He was giving me a look that didn't exactly invite me to keep on giving Mum a hard time. But I was too wound up to back down now.

'Mum, I don't want you speaking to me at all in school – or acting like you know me, OK?'

'Fine,' Mum said. 'That suits me too. I mean, it would be so embarrassing if the other teachers saw us together . . .' She started to smirk.

Quite often when Mum's teasing she does it with such a straight face that you don't realize she *is* only teasing until you've started to take her seriously. Then her face cracks and she has a big laugh at your expense. She always wants me to laugh too and if I don't, she goes on about how she hopes I'm not going to turn out like her father, who was renowned for never laughing at anything except this one thing that someone said at a family funeral, when he laughed out loud in the middle of the service.

I didn't laugh when she did today though. 'Mum,

what sort of a teacher *are* you?' I demanded. 'I mean, when you were Deputy Head at your last school, did the kids there *like* you?'

She laughed again. 'Well, so long as they behaved themselves, I never used to insist on it!'

'So how do I know all the kids here aren't going to think you're a really *duff* head teacher and take it out on me?' I blurted, hearing my voice rise up into more of a shriek at the end than I'd intended.

'Daniel . . .' Dad began sternly – because he hates me acting like a drama queen – but this time Mum interrupted *him*.

'Because, Daniel . . .' she said firmly, straightening up her face although her eyes were still smiling, '. . . I am not going to be a duff head teacher, OK?'

There wasn't much I could say in reply to that. I just hoped she was right.

My first day at my new school was one of the scariest I'd ever experienced. For a start there was the size of the place. Mum had driven me past the building before and I'd seen that it was a lot bigger than my primary school, but that hadn't prepared me for the feeling I had now of being lost amongst a herd of strange kids I'd never seen before, most of them bigger than me. If I was the sort of person who had panic attacks I reckon I'd have had one then. As it was, I started to get this tight feeling in my chest when the bell rang and everybody started to move in the same direction all at once.

After we got to our classrooms, I tried to forget about the size of the school and concentrate on being in my new class. That was scary enough since

I didn't know anybody. I know I'm not the bravest person when it comes to introducing myself to new people, but for the whole of that day I really tried to make an effort. I remembered what Mum had told me about how I tend to scowl when I'm nervous and how that doesn't look very friendly. So I kept forcing myself to smile all the time even though I didn't feel like it, and I kept asking people their names even though there were far too many for me to remember, and I knew I was just going to forget them again and be too embarrassed to ask them a second time and have to spend the rest of the term not knowing what anyone else was called.

I also found myself keeping a lookout for Mum.

Mrs Lyle was our English teacher as well as our head of year and English was our last lesson that day. It took me a while to find the right classroom, so I ended up at a table right at the front, right under Mrs Lyle's nose, and I was the only person who didn't have anybody sitting next to them. Mrs Lyle started reading out our names from the register and when she got to mine she paused for a moment and took an extra long look at me, and I knew that the reason she was staring at me was because she knew that I was the head-teacher's kid. And I instantly decided that she wasn't *pleasant* at all.

My eyes were brimming up, which was really silly. It was just that at the start of term at my old school I'd always been surrounded by friends. And even the people who weren't my friends all *knew* me. There I had *belonged*. I know it would have been different this term, starting secondary school and everything, but I would still have known lots of the other kids. Nearly all of us from my primary school were going to the same secondary school. I'd have been able to call in for Mark on the way to school just like I'd always done. And at school I'd have met up with Kirsty. Our teacher had made her swap seats with Mark last year because she thought I might not talk to her as much as I did to Mark, except I had done and we'd become pretty good friends. She had been going to Disneyland this summer and she'd been going to bring all her photos to show everybody on the first day of term.

Suddenly someone else arrived at the door. It was the girl from the library. She looked different in school uniform and the side bits of her hair were fastened back neatly in a clasp, but it was definitely her. She was mumbling something about having just been transfered to this class and Mrs Lyle was nodding as if she already knew about it and telling her to hurry up and take a seat. And, of course, the only remaining seat was the one next to mine. *Abby*. That was her name. I could tell she recognized me by the way she scowled when she got to our desk.

It seemed idiotic not to say something like, 'Hi again,' or, 'Do you remember me from the other day?' Just sitting there as if we'd never seen each other before seemed more awkward than actually stating the obvious.

But it wasn't until nearly the end of the lesson, by which time Mrs Lyle had told me off twice for fidgeting in my seat and once for fiddling with my rubber and knocking it on to the floor, that I finally got some words to come out of my mouth. 'Hi,' I whispered. 'Did you get a good book out of the library the other day?'

Abby turned to look at me, but before she could answer, Mrs Lyle's loud voice boomed out from the back of the class where she'd gone to look at somebody's book. 'DANIEL! Do you have something you wish to *share* with us?'

'No, miss,' I gulped, twisting my head round to face her.

'It's *missus*,' Abby whispered. '*Missus* Lyle. She's got a thing about it.'

Mrs Lyle was just opening her mouth, presumably to tell me herself that she had a thing about it, when the bell rang.

'My big sister used to have her for English,' Abby added under her breath. 'She says she's got ears like a bat. You have to be careful.'

'You're quite right, Abigail. I *have* got ears like a bat,' Mrs Lyle announced tartly, making Abby jump. 'And *everybody* in this class will do well to remember that.'

As everybody scraped back their chairs ready to make a dash for home, Mrs Lyle looked for an instant like she might be about to yell at us that *her* permission – and not the school bell's – should be our signal to leave the room. Then she waved us out impatiently instead. Mum says teachers find it as much of a struggle as we do to adjust to starting school again after the summer holidays and, right then, Mrs Lyle looked like she'd had enough for one day.

I know *I* had.

It was when we were out in the playground that

a boy from my class spoke to me. I knew his name was Calum because Mrs Lyle had kept having to say it during the lesson to get him to stop talking to his friends. 'Hey, Daniel . . . Is it true your mum's the new head teacher?' he asked, grinning.

I felt my stomach flip over. So far nobody had mentioned that. I could feel the flush I always get when I'm embarrassed creeping up my neck. I loosened my tie.

'Well, is she?'

'Yeah,' I mumbled.

'What's she like then?' Calum was glancing over his shoulder to make sure his audience was appreciating this. 'Is she any good?'

'At what?' I snapped.

I knew as soon as I said it that I shouldn't have. It sounded superior, a put-down, which was of course how I'd meant it, only I shouldn't have said it out loud, not on my first day at a new school, not if I wanted to fit in. I knew I had to say something else quickly, something that would stop them from starting to dislike me.

'I mean, she's not bad at being a mum,' I gushed, 'but I can't vouch for what she's like as a head.' I pulled what I hoped was the right sort of grimace to go along with it – a grimace that was meant to convey that, if she turned out to be a right pain of a head teacher, I'd be on their side rather than hers.

There was a brief silence. The other kids were looking at Calum.

'Well, she can't be any worse than the head teacher we had at primary,' he said. 'She was a real pain. Even the other teachers didn't like her.'

29

His friends started agreeing with him and talking heatedly about their old headmistress.

'See you,' I said quickly, hurrying to get away from them before they started asking me any more questions.

Abby had slipped by while we were standing there and it turned out that she walked home the same way I did. I saw her in front of me as soon as I got out of the school gate. At first I thought I might catch up with her, but she was walking just fast enough to keep the same distance ahead of me the whole time.

When I was almost home, I passed a couple of girls about the same age as me getting off a bus at the stop near my house. They were wearing different school uniforms so they obviously went to the other secondary school near here – the one I had begged to go to when we'd first arrived. They were shouting after Abby, who had already passed the bus stop.

'Your mum's a nutter! My dad says she should be locked up!'

'Yeah! She's killed off all her brain cells with booze!'

They both started laughing.

I hurried past them too, keeping my eyes fixed straight ahead. I felt a bit sick inside, almost as if they were shouting that stuff at me.

'So how was your first day?' Dad asked as he opened the door to me.

'OK,' I said quickly. I just wanted to forget about school now that I was back home again.

Fortunately, Martha joined us in the hallway before Dad could ask any more questions. 'Daddy's taking us to get ice creams. Can I have a whirly ice cream with a flake, Daddy?' She grabbed hold of Dad's hand to drag him towards the door.

'I expect so,' Dad said. He told me to hurry up and get changed out of my uniform. Mum wouldn't be back until later so there was no point in waiting for her.

In the car, Martha wouldn't stop talking about all the things she had done at school. She'd had a much better time than me, by the sound of it, and at playtime she had played with Sally, her new friend from singing class. 'Sally's mum is going to call our mum to see if I can go there to tea next week,' she added proudly.

I was trying not to feel irritated. I just wished I could make friends as easily as Martha, that was all. 'So what's your new teacher like?' I asked, to stop her going on about how nice Sally was.

'She's very nice too,' Martha gushed, 'and she has a cat and guess what he's called . . .' She gave me about two seconds to guess before adding, 'He's called *Felix*.' And she gave a little giggle as if that was a very funny and original name for a cat.

'That's the same name as the cat food,' I told her. 'She's just copied it from there.'

'No she hasn't!' Martha was in the back seat behind me and she leaned forward against her seat belt to jab my shoulder.

I twisted round and reached behind to jab her back, but Dad poked me in the leg instead. 'Stop it, both of you! Either you both sit still and stop arguing or nobody's getting any ice cream except me!'

Martha sat very still after that with her nose squashed against the window as she looked out, and I told her she looked like a little piggy with a snout. I don't know why I kept wanting to annoy her this afternoon.

Dad said, 'What did I just say to you, Daniel?' in his sternest, most about-to-confiscate-ice-creams sort of voice, so I didn't say anything else, but I started to fidget in my seat, tugging at my seat belt and opening and closing the glove compartment a couple of times before I caught Dad glaring at me and stopped. I felt all restless and wound up inside and I couldn't seem to find any way of letting it out except by fiddling with things.

We were nearly at the sea now. 'There it is!' I yelled, feeling momentarily awed. It felt really weird to be driving down a main road full of shops and see-ing the sea at the end of it. We turned at the end of the road and drove along the seafront for a bit, star-ing at all the different people.

When we had parked and got out of the car, there were all these tourists and foreign students walking about, and it felt really strange to be stand-ing outside the shops, tripping over seagulls. For a few moments I allowed myself to imagine that this was only a seaside vacation and we were all going home again at the end of the week. I could even see myself – in a cosy parallel life – buying a rude post-card to send to Uncle Robert and a stick of rock to take back for Mark. I felt a bit better while I was pretending that.

Dad took us to buy the towels Mum had asked him to get for our new bathroom. I didn't see why we needed new towels. There was nothing wrong with our old ones except they didn't match our new bathroom, but since our new bathroom was a horrible lilac colour I didn't see why we'd want them to match.

Finally Dad said we could go and get our ice creams, so we went and got whirly ones with flakes in them and ate them on the pier. It was sunny.

'Daddy, how do they make rock?' Martha asked, as we passed a shop on the pier that was full of the stuff. Martha is always asking questions about things that nobody else would bother about. Normally I think that's OK since she's only seven but that day I just wanted to tell her not to be so dumb.

'Sugar, Martha. Lots of it!' Dad was saying. 'More than enough to rot all your teeth and pull out a few fillings besides.'

'We don't have any fillings,' I grunted.

'Exactly,' Dad replied. 'And have I ever allowed you to eat rock? No!' He rubbed his hands together gleefully. 'Gosh, I'm a good parent!'

Martha giggled as he went to steal a lick from her ice cream, but the funny mixture of feelings inside me seemed to get even stronger and even more mixed up when he said that. It felt so safe having Dad here to look after us and tease us and tell us off when we weren't being nice to each other that I suddenly felt really *furious* with him for going away at the end of the week. And knowing that I needed him so much and that he was *still* going away made me feel even angrier.

'If you were a good parent, you wouldn't be going off and leaving us just when everything's all new and horrible,' I blurted out, tossing my ice cream on to the ground, where it landed upside down on the wooden slats of the pier.

Dad looked surprised. If I'd done that in front of Mum she'd have gone ballistic. She might have even given me a smack, even though she's always saying that it's unwise to smack children outside in case someone sees you and reports you to social services.

'Pick that up and put it in the bin,' Dad said in a low voice. '*Now.*'

I picked up the cone, but the blob of ice cream just stayed there, and Martha started to giggle. She soon stopped when she noticed the look on Dad's face though. We left the pier in silence. When we had almost reached the car, Martha asked if she could go and play on the beach and Dad nodded. She was still eating her ice cream, carefully controlling the drips with her tongue. I was starting to feel a bit sheepish. After all, I must have looked pretty much like a toddler having a tantrum to anyone who'd been looking just now. Martha's ice cream looked really yummy and I really wished I hadn't thrown mine away.

On the beach, while Martha was searching for the best pebbles to throw into the water, Dad began talking to me quietly. 'Daniel, if you knew that Mum or I were going to die soon, would you want to see us again first?'

I flushed. 'Of course I would, but—'

'But you don't think it's so important for me to see *my* mother again?'

I flushed even more. 'It's just not the same . . .'

'Isn't it? Daniel, if you think grown-ups don't still love their parents, then you're wrong. We might not need them in the same way that children do, but it's still a very big deal when we lose them. I really want to see my mother again and say goodbye to her properly before she dies – and *that's* why I'm going to New Zealand on Saturday, even though I know it's not the best time as far as you and Martha and Mum are concerned. OK?'

I swallowed. Dad had never spoken to me quite like this before – as if he wanted me to understand something like *I* was a grown-up. He wasn't angry. He just looked worried. And suddenly I understood that he was worried about his mother *and* worried about us because we *all* needed him now. And nobody could be in two places at the same time. Not even Superman.

'I wish we could just cut you in half,' I sniffed. 'Then you could stay with us *and* go and see Grandma.'

Dad put his arm round me. 'Listen, Daniel,' he said softly. 'It's only for a few weeks, and Mum's still going to be here.'

'I know,' I mumbled, burying my face in his jumper and hugging him. I didn't know why I felt as bad as this about Dad going. Except that Dad never went away.

'Daniel, are you crying?' Martha called out.

I pulled away from Dad and glared at her. '*No!*'

'You look like you are!' She was starting to pick her way across the pebbles towards us.

'Come on,' Dad shouted, clapping me on the

back. 'The last one back to the car has to do all the dishes tonight!' And he began to stride across the stony beach in the wrong direction, making out that he'd totally forgotten where he'd left the car.

I got back first, Martha was second – giggling like mad – and Dad came in last.

'*You've* got to do the dishes, Daddy!' Martha shouted gleefully.

'Hey, I thought I said the last one back to the car *doesn't* have to do them!' he protested.

'No, you didn't!' Martha and I both dived at him and started tickling him, one under each arm, until he gave in. And as I sat in the back seat as we drove home, so that Martha could have a turn in the front, I decided I was going to do my best not to cry or make a big fuss when we took him to the airport in three days' time. Instead, I was going to act like a grown-up, so that he'd be proud of me.

4

It was the grown-ups who started crying first when we took Dad to the airport. Mum didn't even get as far as the check-in desk before she was flinging her arms round Dad, saying, 'Oh, Malcolm, I know you have to go, but I wish you didn't!' And then she was crying and kissing Dad and he was kissing and hugging her back which was really embarrassing since they were standing in the middle of the check-in area and everyone was having to wheel their trollies around them. Dad pulled back from her and that's when I saw that he was crying too. At least, his eyes had gone all watery and he was fishing about in his pocket like he was searching for a tissue.

Martha waited until we got to the entrance to the departure area before she started blubbing. She kissed him goodbye nicely enough and then, when he started to walk away from us, she ran after him and Mum had to go and prise her away while she wailed, 'Don't go, Daddy!'

I was the only one who managed not to cry.

Martha was still sobbing as she walked between Mum and me back to the short-stay car park. 'Martha, listen . . .' I said, putting on my most grown-up voice 'If *Dad* was going to die soon, *you'd* want to go and see him again, wouldn't you?'

'Is Daddy going to die?' Martha gasped.

'For God's sake, Daniel!' Mum snapped. She turned to Martha. 'Of course not, darling. Nobody's going to die.'

'Except Grandma,' I reminded them.

Mum glared at me again.

On the way home, Mum tried to cheer Martha up by offering to stop and get her an ice cream. When that didn't work, she suggested we went to the pet shop right now to choose the goldfish Dad had promised to buy Martha when he got back.

Martha stopped crying pretty quickly and started to choose names for her goldfish.

I started to feel worse, though. Now that Dad was gone, there didn't seem much point in being brave any more, since I'd mainly been doing it for his sake. I waited for Mum to come up with an ice-cream-and-goldfish equivalent to cheer *me* up, but she didn't. I guess she thought I was too old to need it.

A few days later I had my first close encounter with Mum in school. So far I had seen her only in assembly. The Year Sevens had assembly twice a week. Sometimes Mum took it and sometimes it was the deputy head. I had cringed in my seat the first time Mum had taken it, but she hadn't said much except welcomed us to the school and read out some announcements. A few of the kids in my class had looked at me when she started speaking and I was glad I'd persuaded her to wear her soft green woollen suit instead of the horrible brown one which makes her look frumpy. I had reminded myself to tell her that she didn't look fat at all in that green suit, except for maybe just a little bit round the hips.

The day started off badly when Mrs Lyle gave us back the essays we'd handed in at the start of term – the ones we were supposed to have done over the summer. I had spent forty minutes on mine the night before it was meant to be handed in – I'd just never been able to take it seriously right from the start – and I should have known I'd live to regret it.

'Daniel MacKenzie!' Mrs Lyle paused as she sailed up and down the aisles dropping English exercise books on desks with a flick of her big bony wrist. 'This is not what I would term – or indeed what *most* teachers in this school would term – an essay.' The way she said *most* made me wonder if she was having a dig at Mum – insinuating that Mum must have let my essay pass as an essay in order for me to have given it in like that. 'I would call it a paragraph,' Mrs Lyle continued, as some of the other kids started to snigger. 'And a fairly short paragraph at that. Would you care to read it out to us, Daniel?'

I froze. My mouth had gone dry. I felt like my throat had turned into a huge lump of concrete and I didn't see how I could squeeze any words through it even if my life depended on it.

'Well?' From the look Mrs Lyle was giving me I was starting to think that my life *did* depend on it. After what seemed like an eternity, she said, 'All right then. Perhaps it might be a good idea if you redid it and this time wrote something that you wouldn't be too ashamed to read out to the rest of the class.'

I nodded, gratefully closing my exercise book as she picked on someone else.

At my old school we'd once had to write essays imagining we were loaves of bread and my teacher had joked that my imaginary encounter with a bread-slicer was the most spine-chilling of the lot and that maybe I should become a writer of horror fiction when I grew up. After that she'd always written little encouraging comments at the bottom of my essays like, '*Well done! Another surprise ending!*' or '*Great story but I could hardly read some of it – watch the handwriting!*'

I felt like I had turned into a different person here – someone who wasn't popular with the teachers at all and who couldn't write *anything*.

'Right, all of you,' Mrs Lyle said loudly. 'I have to leave the classroom for about twenty minutes and while I'm gone I want you to read quietly. No talking. Those of you who haven't got books can choose one from the reading box at the back of the room. Our new head teacher, Mrs MacKenzie, is in the room next door, filling in for Miss Barnes, who's off sick today. I've asked her to listen out for any noise. So make sure there isn't any!'

I felt like my stomach had been yanked upwards and rammed against the lump of concrete in my throat. Mum was next door. Mum was going to come in and tell us off if there was any noise. The thought of it made me want to throw up. Especially as she was wearing her horrible brown suit today – the one that made her look really strait-laced and schoolmarmish. And I hadn't checked this morning to see if she was wearing some decent shoes or the clumpy ones she sometimes wears when she thinks she's going to be on her feet all day.

As soon as Mrs Lyle had gone, lots of people in the class started to whisper. Some pulled out books to read. I started flicking my rubber about my desk. Calum – the boy who had asked me about Mum on my first day – came and stood directly behind me. I froze, feeling my lips go dry as I waited to hear what he was going to say now. But he wasn't there to speak to me. He was after Abby.

'Hey, Abigail . . . What did you write for your essay? *On the first day of my summer holidays my mum said, "I know, let's go to the pub. You can have a can of Coke while I knock back a bottle or two of whisky . . ."*'

'Shut it, Calum,' Abby snapped, jumping up and heading for the back of the room to join the people who were congregating around a large cardboard box full of books.

I got up quietly and followed her. I know it was pretty cowardly of me, but I couldn't help being a bit relieved that Calum was picking on Abby instead of me.

'Hey, I picked that up first!' Abby protested as Calum slipped up behind her and snatched the book she was holding from her hand.

'So?' Calum teased. 'You should've held on to it tighter, shouldn't you? The way your mum holds on to her whisky bottle!'

Some of the others sniggered and Abby's face went bright red. 'GIVE!' she snarled, trying to grab the book back.

'MAKE ME!' Calum was laughing. A few other people started to laugh too. I secretly prayed for them to be quiet. The last thing I wanted was for Mum to hear us. Why had Mum promised Mrs Lyle that she'd listen out for us when she *knew* this was my class? It wasn't fair! She'd *promised* me she wouldn't embarrass me! How did she think I'd feel if she marched in and started yelling at us?

'Hey, Daniel, get out the way!' Calum was shoving me to one side to get back to his seat.

'That book is really boring,' I told him, which was the truth. I'd got it out of the library last summer and it had taken me ages to get through it because there were loads of boring descriptions of mountains and stuff, and hardly any bits where people said things. Those are my favourite bits in books – the 'direct speech', Mum calls it. I can just whizz through books when I like the characters and they talk a lot.

'Oh yeah?' Calum obviously didn't appreciate my piece of advice. 'Why are you saying that? Are you Abby's boyfriend or something?'

I blushed. 'No . . . It's just—'

'Hey? Is your mum a boozer too? Is that why you're palling up with Abby?' He grinned. 'Oh no – your mummy is the headmistress, isn't she? All prim and proper but a bit fat, I reckon.' He looked round for support. 'What do you lot think? Could our new head teacher do with losing a bit, do you reckon?'

I blushed even more. I was about to say something back when I suddenly noticed that the rest of the class had gone silent.

I looked up. Mum was standing at the front of

the room, staring straight at me and Calum. 'IS THERE A PROBLEM BACK THERE?'

I froze. I found my eyes focusing on her tummy, which is the bit of her that sticks out the most.

Everyone rushed back to their seats. I headed for my desk too. Mum shifted her gaze to encompass the whole class as she began to lecture us about the noise. Her tone of voice was just like the one she uses at home when she's telling me off about something. It felt weird. I don't know why, but somehow I hadn't expected her to seem like the same person in school.

'. . . so if anyone here can read and talk at the same time, I'd be more than happy to see a demonstration!' she concluded briskly. 'Well? Any takers?'

Nobody made a sound.

'Right then! I want to see all noses in books! Next door we're in the middle of reading a very romantic scene from *Romeo and Juliet*, and I won't be in such a good mood if I have to interrupt it to come in here and tell you again!'

At least she didn't seem to have a problem controlling the class. She was being pretty cool as a matter of fact. Much cooler than I'd expected. Even if her tummy was enormous.

5

It was the following day when Mum woke up with a rash and said she thought it was a side effect of the lithium so she was going to stop taking it for a few days.

'But maybe it's measles or something,' I said when she told me at breakfast time. I was swinging on my chair again, which Mum usually hates, but this morning she was too distracted to notice.

'Don't be silly, Daniel. This is an allergic rash. I've been thinking I should cut down the number of tablets I take anyway. If you ask me, this is a sign that I was right.'

'Let's phone Dad and ask him what to do,' I suggested, banging my chair down and looking at my watch. It would be eight in the evening in New Zealand, so it would be all right to phone.

'He won't be able to tell me what the rash is, if he can't see it,' Mum snapped. 'No, I'll just stop the tablets and see if it goes away.'

'Shouldn't you ask the doctor before you do that?' I asked. 'Maybe it's not the tablets. Maybe you're allergic to something else. Mark's dad came out in a rash once after he'd eaten lobster.'

'I haven't eaten any lobster.'

'No, but you might have eaten something else.'

Mum sighed. 'I suppose I could phone up and ask if that doctor I saw at the clinic could fit me in.' She meant the psychiatry clinic.

I nodded encouragingly.

She came off the phone looking a bit fed up. The doctor had told her she should not on any account stop her lithium and that he'd take a look at the rash himself if she could just pop up to the hospital where he was going to be spending all day doing a ward round.

'It must be a really big ward if it takes him all day,' I said.

'Psychiatrists take all day to do everything,' Mum said, sounding irritated. 'They don't go round the ward seeing everyone. Oh no! They summon you into a room and ask you loads of questions and it's not just you and them either. Everyone else in the team is there gawping at you and reporting on every movement you've made in the last twenty-four hours. Do you know, they have a thing they call a sleep chart? The nurses come and stand at the end of your bed every hour during the night to see if your eyes are open or not. If you close them, they tick you off as being asleep. Isn't that pathetic? I used to lie awake all night sometimes, with my eyes closed, and the nurses would tell the doctor that I was sleeping very well.'

'Did *you* tell the doctor you hadn't really slept?' I asked, listening with interest. Mum had never told me anything before about the times she'd been a psychiatric patient. It was sort of like a taboo subject in our house. Dad always got really stony faced if

I brought the subject up, and he'd told me a number of times that it was grown-up business that he didn't think I needed to know any more about than what he'd already told me. Which wasn't much.

'Sometimes,' Mum replied. 'Sometimes it suited me not to tell him anything.'

I suddenly registered something. 'Mum, you're not sleeping very well *now*.' Ever since we'd moved here, she had been complaining on and off about having trouble getting to sleep.

'Oh, don't *you* start, Daniel!' Mum walked away from me huffily.

Since it was a school day Mum had to phone up and say she would be late in. She also told her secretary to tell my registration teacher that I would be late in too. 'I want you to come with me, Daniel,' she said. 'You don't mind, do you? We can drop Martha off at school on the way.'

'You usually go to outpatients on your own,' I replied, surprised. Normally, Mum doesn't like me taking time off school for anything.

'I know, but this isn't outpatients in the general hospital, Daniel. The only way the doctor can see me today is if I go up to the psychiatric hospital. I don't like going into those places on my own.'

I stared at her. I was remembering now, years ago, when she was admitted to a psychiatric hospital. That was before Martha was born, a couple of months before Mum was due to have her. I couldn't remember much about it. We'd had a nanny, whose name I can't remember, come and live with us for a while after that. I don't know how long it was before

I saw Mum again, but I know it was a pretty long time.

After we'd dropped Martha off at school, I started to read out the directions Mum had been given by the doctor's secretary. The psychiatric hospital was an old building which looked a bit dilapidated from the outside.

'God, it's one of those old bins,' Mum said as we drove in though the gate.

I asked her what she meant.

'Bins – like rubbish bins. Where they put mentally ill people. At least, they did in the old days. Do you know, Daniel, years ago people used to live their whole lives in these places and never be let out?' She shuddered.

'Yes, but they let people out now, don't they?'

'Of course. Otherwise I wouldn't be here, would I?' She laughed, but in a hollow sort of way as if she was only joking to cover up some other feelings that she had inside.

I wished Dad was here.

After we'd parked the car, I followed Mum up to the main doors. 'It looks a bit like the library,' I said, trying to cheer us both up. 'The building, I mean. Maybe they were built at the same time.'

Mum didn't reply. She didn't look like she was listening. She walked up to a man who was sitting at the reception desk behind a glass window in the entrance hall.

'I'm here to see Doctor White,' she said. 'Isobel MacKenzie.'

'If you'd just like to take a seat over there.'

We went and sat on some chairs which had cracked plastic covering with the foam showing. While we were sitting there an elderly man whose clothes looked too big for him shuffled past smoking a cigarette.

'It says, *No Smoking*,' I whispered to Mum, pointing to the sign on the wall.

'Shush, Daniel,' Mum said. There were little beads of sweat above her top lip, even though it wasn't hot.

I can never sit still in waiting rooms for very long, so I stood up and went to look at the pictures on the opposite wall. They had been painted by patients. They weren't very good.

'Mrs Mackenzie.' The receptionist called her over. 'Doctor White will see you now if you'd like to go up to his office. You go up those stairs to the first floor, turn right and follow the signs to Elizabeth Ward. His office is just through the swing doors.'

Mum nodded. She came back over to me. 'I think you should stay here, Daniel. I won't be long.' She leaned in closer and whispered to me, 'Did he say turn right *after* the swing doors?'

'Up the stairs, then turn right, then go through the swing doors,' I told her. 'I'll come with you if you want.'

She didn't need much persuasion to let me take her, which was just as well, because when we got to the first floor she couldn't remember which floor he'd said. I reckoned she must have forgotten because she was nervous. There were two seats outside Dr White's office, so I sat down while Mum

48

knocked on his door. I heard him say, 'Come in!' and Mum disappeared inside.

I started to look round. The corridor where I was sitting led to the ward. I knew that the patients here didn't lie in their beds all day like they do in ordinary hospitals. Their bodies were OK. It was their minds that were sick.

The doors of the ward swung open suddenly and three women – who could have been patients except that they looked too normal – started walking towards me. They were talking and smiling. One of them glanced at me as they passed, but that was all.

I sat staring at the sign on the wall opposite. It said HOSPITAL CHAPEL, with an arrow pointing down the corridor away from the ward. I remembered Mum saying once that even though she wasn't very religious, churches always made her feel safe. I wished I could feel safer than I did right now. I know it was silly, but I kept having to fight the urge to look right and left all the time in case some mad person came running up to attack me. I couldn't believe that Mum had once been a mad person, though I'm sure she wasn't ever the sort of mad person who attacked people. I had never been allowed to see her when she was like that. Dad had only taken me to visit her in hospital when she was nearly better and I couldn't even remember much about that.

'Gotta light?'

I jumped. A woman with long grey hair was approaching me from the ward. She was wearing her cardigan inside out and she had a green hat on her head that looked like it came from a jumble sale. It was difficult to tell her age. When she smiled at me, her teeth were all missing. She had a wrinkled face and she kept coughing. She was clutching a plastic bag.

I shook my head to let her know that I didn't have a light, but she stopped to talk to me anyway. 'You on this ward?'

'No.'

'You ever killed a cat?'

'No.'

'They were living in my loft.'

I gulped. 'Pardon?'

'People. Killing cats in my loft. Had to wear earplugs at night so I couldn't hear them.'

I felt a bit queasy as she sat down on the spare seat beside me. Surely Mum couldn't ever have been like that. The woman leaned towards me and peered at my face. Her breath smelt of cigarettes. I stood up abruptly and headed speedily down the corridor away from her. I pushed through one set of swing doors, then another set, and found myself in a large room where a television was blaring away in the background. The room was full of cigarette smoke and everybody was slouched around the TV. A few of the people in the room turned to stare at me. One of the women had long dark hair and from the back she looked a bit like Mum.

I stumbled out into the corridor again, back in the direction I'd come from. The cat lady wasn't anywhere in sight, thank goodness. Mum and Dr White came out of his office just as I was panicking about whether or not I was back in the right passageway. Dr White was a tall thin man with curly hair. He was younger than I'd expected him to be.

Mum was clutching a piece of paper which, even though I was halfway along the corridor from her, I recognized as a prescription.

'Daniel, what are you doing down there?' Mum called out.

'Nothing,' I mumbled, hurrying to join them.

Dr White looked concerned. 'Are you all right?'

I gulped. 'Yeah.'

He put his hand on my shoulder. He reminded me a bit of Dad when he did that. 'Some of the patients here are very poorly and they might behave a bit strangely. Did one of them give you a fright?'

'No,' I tried to look chilled, adding, 'There was a lady going on about killing cats.'

'Well, she's poorly too. Don't worry. She hasn't really killed any cats.'

'It wasn't *her* she said was killing them. It was the people in her loft.'

Dr White nodded like he wasn't hearing anything new or anything particularly concerning. Or maybe he just didn't rate cats. 'I've had a look at your mum, Daniel. That rash is nothing to worry about and I've given her something to stop the itch.' He smiled at her. 'OK, Isobel?'

Mum nodded. 'Thanks again.' She turned to me. 'Come on, Daniel. We'll go to the chemist and then we'd better both be getting to school.'

We said goodbye and left.

I should have asked what he'd told her to do about the lithium, but I forgot. I was too busy trying to make sense of what I'd just seen on the ward. Was that how Mum had been when I was little? Had she been like those people in there?

'Mum, I don't like this hospital much,' I told her as we passed through the reception area where the receptionist was talking to a loud man who had his nose pressed right up against the glass partition. 'Even if it does help people get better.'

'I don't like it either.' Mum shuddered.

'Don't worry, Mum,' I said. 'I wouldn't ever let anyone put you in here, no matter how sick you got.'

'If I was very sick you might not have a choice,' Mum said lightly.

'Yes I would,' I said, putting my arm round her protectively. 'I wouldn't let *anyone*, no matter what. Not even Dad.' I don't know why I added that.

'Oh, Daniel!' Mum smiled, shaking her head at me. She grabbed hold of my hand suddenly. 'Come on. Let's run.'

And the two of us ran back to the car together, laughing, because she was escaping with me and not staying behind inside that horrible, scary building.

6

The next two weeks were weird. I couldn't get used to Dad not being there in the evenings and I knew Mum was really missing him too. I knew because she ran to the phone every time it rang in case it was him – even when the time difference meant it wasn't likely to be since Dad would have to be phoning in the middle of the night at his end. New Zealand was twelve hours ahead of us. Before he left, Dad had said he'd ring us every two or three days to see how we were getting on, but in those first two weeks he was ringing us almost every day. He sounded really close on the phone, not like he was across the other side of the world at all. He told us a little bit about what was going on at his end – Grandma was very poorly now – but mostly he just wanted to hear about us.

Mum had started bringing lots of paperwork home with her and was doing it after Martha and I were in bed. That wasn't new. Dad was always having to tell her off for working too hard. But now Mum seemed to be staying up half the night judging by the times I'd woken up and seen the downstairs light still on. Often it was three or four in the morning.

On the Sunday night, after I woke up to use the bathroom, I went downstairs to see what Mum was doing. I found her sitting at the dining table with a mug of coffee, surrounded by bits of paper. She was in her pyjamas and dressing gown, so she'd obviously intended to go to bed at some point. Her hair was all messy as if she'd been running her hands through it.

'Are you OK, Mum?' I asked her.

Mum looked up, starting slightly at the sight of me standing there. 'God, Daniel, don't creep up on me like that!'

'I wasn't *creeping*.'

'Well, you gave me a fright!' She sounded wide awake.

'Sorry. Mum, why aren't you in bed?'

'I can't sleep so I'm making a list of ideas to raise funds for the school. You know they've got this annual book sale that your Mrs Lyle keeps going on about . . . well, I think we should vamp it up a bit.'

I didn't know what *vamp* meant.

'Look it up in the dictionary, Daniel,' Mum said when I asked her. She handed me the one that just happened to be sitting on the table. (Even at four in the morning she can't stop being a teacher.)

'Vamp . . . *to improvise inartistically or crudely,*' I read out. I wasn't sure what *improvise* meant either, but I couldn't be bothered looking that up as well. Besides, *inartistically* and *crudely* pretty much gave me the picture. 'Don't you think Mrs Lyle might be a bit offended if you just take over like that?' I asked her.

'Mrs Lyle is a very competent teacher, but she's very dull, Daniel. She has dull ideas. So do a lot of the other staff. They mean well enough, but they're so *boring*. If you ask me, the whole school needs livening up a bit.'

I couldn't believe she was criticizing my teachers. Normally she's always saying that teachers do a really tough job and they don't get the respect for it – or the salary – that they deserve.

'Back to bed, Daniel,' she said. 'Go on. You've got school tomorrow. I don't want you nodding off in class. I used to hate that when I taught English. I never knew if the kids who fell asleep were just sleep-deprived or if I was *boring* them unconscious.' She started to laugh.

I could still hear her laughing as I climbed the stairs. It sounded a bit weird in the middle of the night.

I was seething as I walked home the following day. I had agreed to stay in the school library doing my homework until half-past five so that I wouldn't get home before Mum did. But I hadn't agreed that she could come and find me when she was ready to leave, and call out in this really mumsy voice, '*Sweetheart, do you want a lift home?*'

She said afterwards that she hadn't realized anyone else was in the library at the time because the older boy who'd been studying there had just gone to put a book back. I felt really angry with her. What if that boy repeated what he'd heard? Everyone in my class might find out and start making fun of me. *Calum* might find out.

I had stubbornly refused a lift, so she had gone off to fetch Martha.

I was dawdling because I was in no hurry to get home, when I saw the two girls I'd seen yelling at Abby on my first day. They were sitting on the wall at the bus stop. Their school blazers were tossed on the ground on top of their school bags and their ties were hanging loose around their necks. Abby was standing at the bus stop too. She had changed out of her uniform and she was obviously waiting for a bus. The girls were goading her about her mum again.

'So how much does she drink then? Two bottles a night . . . ? Three . . . ? Does she know her liver's gonna pack up if she doesn't stop?'

I could have walked straight past. After all, Abby hadn't been all that friendly to me so far. But something about the way she was standing there looking so humiliated stopped me.

'Hi, Abby.' It was all I could think of to say at such short notice.

She looked at me as if she didn't know if I was her saviour or someone who was about to start having a go at her too. I pretended I couldn't hear the comments the other girls were making. ('Oh, look. She's got a little boyfriend. Isn't that sweet?')

'Where are you going?' I asked Abby.

'My friend's,' she grunted. 'I have *got* some, you know.'

I ignored that. After all, *I* hadn't said anything about her having no friends at school, had I? She ought to know that I'd be the *last* person to bring that up. 'What time's the bus?' I glanced down at my watch. It was now nearly six.

'Dunno. I think I must have just missed one.'

'Right.' We both stood looking in the direction the bus was meant to come from. 'If you like you can come round to mine instead,' I offered in a rush. 'Mum won't mind. She's probably not even back yet.'

Abby bit her lip, glancing over at the girls, who weren't showing any signs of leaving. She looked down the street again, but there was still no bus. 'OK,' she said quickly.

We walked side by side away from the bus stop, with the two girls shouting after us. 'Who *are* they?' I asked when we'd turned the corner.

'We went to the same primary school. They know about my mum.' She flushed.

Her embarrassment made me feel embarrassed too and, before I knew it, I had blurted out, 'You mean about her drinking?' I don't know why I always have to come right out with things like that. 'I won't tell anyone else,' I mumbled quickly.

'Everyone else knows anyway,' she said. 'I wanted to start at a secondary school where the other kids didn't know about Mum, so I asked to go to this one. It's not the one the rest of my primary school were going to, but it's where my big sister went. But it turns out that a girl who was in my class last year is Calum's cousin, so he found out really quickly.' She sighed. 'So I may as well not have bothered switching schools. I may as well have just gone to the same one as everybody else. At least I had some friends who were going there as well as the people who picked on me.'

'Sorry.' I didn't know what else to say. Now I understood why she didn't seem to know any more people at school than I did. 'You can still come back to my place,' I said. 'If you don't want to go home right now, I mean.'

'It's OK,' she said. 'My sister should be back from work soon anyhow. I'll ring my friend and tell her.'

'OK.' I hadn't really expected her to come back with me, but I couldn't help feeling a bit disappointed just the same. It would have been nice to start making a friend my own age here. A car horn tooted at me and I saw it was Mum driving past with Martha, who she must have just picked up from her after-school club. 'Well, see you tomorrow then,' I said, turning to Abby.

She was already walking away, but she lifted her hand to wave to me as she called back, 'See ya!' I stood watching her leave, thinking that from the back she reminded me a bit of my friend Kirsty from my old school. Kirsty had walked home with Mark and me sometimes. Abby paused to kick an empty can out of the gutter and started to dribble it along the pavement. That wasn't like Kirsty. Kirsty used to hate it when Mark and I went on about football all the time.

When I got in, Mum was heading across the hall, her arms piled high with books and sheets of paper. 'Those other teachers are getting to be a real pain,' she grumbled as I followed her into the kitchen. 'One useless opinion after another! I'm telling you, if I have to listen one more time to Margaret Lyle's pathetic plan for her dreary book sale or the deputy head droning on about—'

'Mum, maybe you shouldn't be *saying* this to

me?' I interrupted her crossly. It made me feel uncomfortable. Besides, she seemed to have totally forgotten about what had happened before in the library. I had expected at least one more apology for that.

'Who else am I going to say it to?' Mum snapped, pushing her hair out of her face and plonking all her stuff down on the kitchen table without even checking to see if we'd wiped it clean from breakfast this morning. Mum was getting much snappier since Dad had left, I'd noticed. She had also started to talk quite a lot about the other teachers at home in a way she never did normally. Like about how the deputy head had bad breath when you got up close to him, and how the head of science, Mr Gregory, kept looking at her legs. I hated it when she said stuff like that about my teachers. I mean, they were my *teachers*, for goodness sake!

I decided to try a different tack. 'If you'd let me go to a different school, you could've moaned about the other teachers as much as you liked. It wouldn't have mattered then, because I wouldn't know them. And what happened just now in the library wouldn't have happened either.' My campaign to get her to let me change schools wasn't completely dead and buried. Last week I'd tried to recruit Martha on to my side by pointing out that in a few years' time, *she'd* have to go to the same school as Mum as well, but she just got all excited and wanted to know if she'd be allowed to eat her school dinner with Mum.

Mum just grinned. 'Still finding me an awful embarrassment, are you?' She opened the door of the fridge and discovered that we had nothing left in it except cheese. She opened the freezer instead. 'Chicken nuggets!' she announced triumphantly. She bounded over to the vegetable rack and pulled out a bag of potatoes. 'How about helping me peel these?'

'Mum, are you stressed?' I asked her. She seemed really tense and sort of hyper-alert or something.

'Quite the opposite!' Mum said. 'I feel full of energy! Ever since I stopped those stupid tablets as a matter of fact. Now, don't use that knife. Use the potato peeler. I've told you before, I don't want chopped fingers in my dinner.'

I stared at her. 'What? The lithium tablets?'

'Of course! I wasn't on any others last time I looked.'

'But you're not meant to stop them,' I protested. 'Dad said. He said you got really ill last time you stopped them.' *Really ill, really quickly*, had been Dad's exact words. That had been when Mum had come off the tablets during her pregnancy with Martha. Dad had explained that much to me when I'd asked why Mum had got sick then. He'd said that Mum had really wanted to have another baby, so she'd decided to stop taking the lithium, because it's risky taking lithium when you're pregnant. There's a chance that it might harm the unborn child. Mum had stayed on the tablets ever since as far as I knew.

'Your dad isn't always right, Daniel. It's time you learned that,' Mum said briskly.

'Well, what about Doctor White?' I asked, starting

to peel a potato. 'What did *he* say? Did *he* say you should keep taking them?'

'Of course he did! You'd think he had shares in the company that makes lithium, the way he was going on about it. Sometimes I think that's how all these doctors earn their living – by being in a conspiracy with the drug companies. I've been telling your father for years that these lithium tablets do more than just make me put on weight, but he won't listen! They slow my mind up too. I know they do. And they must have caused that rash, because as soon as I stopped taking them, it disappeared.'

'But you put that cream on it too,' I pointed out. 'The stuff you got from the chemist.'

'Well, I had to keep him happy, didn't I?' Mum said. 'Doctor White, I mean.'

'But, Mum—'

'And I don't want you telling tales to your father next time he phones. He'll only freak out and insist on coming home and missing his mother on her deathbed and we don't want that, do we?'

I swallowed, feeling even more confused. It was important that Dad got to spend this time with his mother. Dad had told me that himself. But if Mum had stopped her medication . . .

'Daniel, did you know that your father's mother – and the rest of his family – tried to get him to dump me when we were engaged?' Mum suddenly said. 'It was when they found out I'd been in a psychiatric hospital. Your grandmother nearly had a fit when she heard her precious son was going to marry a *mental case*. She called me that once, you know – said it to your dad when she thought I

61

wasn't listening. And when he did marry me, she had to get as far away from me as possible, so she emigrated to New Zealand. I mean, how pathetic is that?'

'Mum . . .' I suddenly felt I shouldn't be listening to this. It just wasn't like Mum to tell me all this. And anyway, I was almost sure that it wasn't true. 'I've still got homework to do, OK?'

I left off peeling the potatoes and went upstairs. Martha's door was open and I could see her sitting on the floor in her bedroom, playing with her toy fire engine.

'Look, Daniel!' she shouted, pointing at her dolls' house. 'That house is on fire and there are ten children inside it. It's a case for . . .' She grinned at me, pointing up at the ceiling as if she could see him coming.

'*Superman!*' I finished, flinging out my arms and swooping wildly around her bedroom, because pretending to be Superman suddenly seemed a whole lot easier than just being me.

7

Mum was right. She didn't get ill like Dad had said she would if she stopped her lithium tablets.

But certain things about her behaviour started to seem a bit odd. She often stayed up half the night now and yet she still seemed wide awake in the mornings. Over the next week she switched from hardly going to the supermarket at all, to going there almost every evening and stocking up on masses of things. She also started buying lots of really expensive chocolates from a delicatessen she had discovered near the school, and was eating her way through at least two boxes a day. When I asked her if she was worried that the chocolates would make her put on weight, she just laughed and said, 'No! Isn't it wonderful?' She seemed very happy about it. She was buying in loads of other stuff which she normally avoided and there was plenty of great food in the house for Martha and me – cakes and biscuits and loads of crisps.

Mum's dress sense seemed to have changed too.

'Mum, you're not wearing *that* to school, are you?' I asked when she came down the stairs one morning wearing a bright yellow cardigan instead of the brown jacket that went with the brown skirt of her horrible frumpy suit.

'I don't know why you're complaining about the way *I'm* dressed,' Mum retorted. 'I mean, look at what *you're* wearing! Talk about dismal!'

'Mum, this is my school uniform!'

'Even your tie is grey. Purple and grey. You look like you're going to a funeral.'

'Yeah . . . well . . .' *School? Funeral?* I mean, what was the difference? (In terms of the solemness of the occasion, I mean.) 'School uniforms are meant to be dull,' I told her.

'Hmm . . .' She didn't sound convinced.

In assembly I thought she looked like a light bulb. I kept waiting for someone else in my class to point that out, but nobody did.

'I have an announcement to make regarding this year's book sale,' she shouted out, and I couldn't help glancing nervously at Mrs Lyle, who was standing at the back of all the Year Sevens. 'Instead of just books,' Mum continued, 'we're going to sell plants and cakes as well. Because books and plants and cakes all go together.'

There were a few funny looks being exchanged in the assembly hall by people who didn't see *how* they went together, but Mum was unphased. 'Instead of having stalls with books on them here in the school hall, we're going to convert the hall into one of those cafe book-shops like they have in America. I'm going to bring in my sofas from home and anyone else who wants to lend sofas or armchairs is most welcome to do so. I've put an advert in the local paper this year as well, so that more people know about it.'

Somebody in my class whispered, 'How are we supposed to bring in *sofas*?' (Which is what I was thinking too.)

Nobody asked me anything about it, thank goodness. The unexpected thing was that lots of people at school seemed to keep forgetting that our headmistress was also my mother. I mean, they all *knew*, and I'd got lots of comments about it at the beginning, but now they often talked about her like you'd talk about any head teacher, even when I was there. It was as if they couldn't hold the two ideas together in their heads at the same time – Mrs MacKenzie, the head teacher, and Mrs MacKenzie, mother of Daniel – so they sort of kept splitting them up.

The only person who didn't split them was Mrs Lyle. We had English straight after assembly and the first thing she said when we'd all settled down was, 'So, everybody . . . who's planning on bringing the odd *sofa* with them when they come to our book sale then?' Everyone laughed, even Abby, and Mrs Lyle added, 'It looks like you'll be the only one, Daniel.'

I went bright red and everyone immediately remembered that I was Daniel *MacKenzie,* who was only masquerading as an ordinary member of the class. I tried to think of something to say in reply. Mrs Lyle obviously resented my mother just barging in and taking over the organization of the book sale and I can't say I blamed her. After all, from the way Mum was carrying on, you'd think Mrs Lyle was incapable of making it a successful event herself. I looked Mrs Lyle in the eyes (which was easy because I was still sitting right at the front of the class) and said, 'Sorry, miss.' Because I really did feel sorry about what Mum was doing and I felt sort of responsible too in a funny sort of way.

Mrs Lyle went bright red herself then and didn't say anything about being a *missus*. She immediately started having a go at somebody else for not doing their homework, and when I accidently banged into the desk behind while I was swinging on my chair a bit later on, she didn't even tell me off for it.

At break-time I'd meant to ask Abby if she wanted to hang out with me, but she left the room so quickly that I didn't have time to. So I did my usual thing of heading for the boys' toilets first to kill a bit of time before going to the tuck shop where, by then, there would always be a longish queue. I could then join the end of it and stand there for most of break without looking awkward because I was on my own. I hated looking like I had nothing to do.

I headed for the stairs, making for the furthest-away toilets because that way the whole trip took up more time. I had to remind myself to walk on the right, which was the rule at my new school to stop everyone bumping into each other. At my last school we had to walk on the left, which is far more sensible, if you ask me, considering that everybody *drives* on the left.

I wasn't really looking where I was going because I was thinking about something that had happened yesterday. Martha had been crayoning a picture of the seaside – a yellow rectangle of beach with a blue strip of sky above it and lots of white 'V' shapes on the sky which were the seagulls. Mum had come along and dripped white blobs of Tipp Ex all over it and written *'Seagull Pooh by Martha MacKenzie'* in big letters along the bottom. It would have been funny except that Martha was really upset because she was meant to hand it in the next day as homework.

I jumped as someone put out their arm and stopped me in my tracks. 'DANIEL!'

It was Mum.

'Go away,' I hissed, quickly scanning the area to see if anyone from my class was around.

'Don't be silly!' Mum said, ruffling my hair before I could squirm out of her reach. 'Can't stop. I'm on my way to do my social bit in the staffroom. See you later. By the way, I thought we could go to the beach after school. It's silly to live by the seaside and never go to the beach, isn't it?' She said the last bit really loudly.

The kids who were within earshot all turned to stare at me and right then I just wanted to die. Or at least hire a contract killer to assassinate Mum.

'It's not fair!' I burst out, sounding like a five year old and not even caring. 'You just go out of your way to embarrass me at school. You do it on purpose!'

'Don't be silly!' Mum said, handing me an ice cream even though I'd just told her I didn't want one. 'Why be embarrassed?'

'It's *normal* to be embarrassed when you've got a mother who makes you look really stupid in front of everyone at school!' I snapped.

We were standing at an ice-cream booth on the seafront. Right now, it was high tide, so there wasn't any sand to play on, but Martha was excited anyway because she'd just got an ice cream that was half vanilla and half strawberry. She frowned as Mum handed me my ice cream, as if she was worried about something. 'Daniel, you're not going to throw that on the floor, are you?'

'Don't be silly, Martha!' Mum said, getting out her purse and paying for them.

'But that's what he did when—' Martha started to say, but Mum had stopped listening.

'Kate!' she shrieked, and before we could stop her she had rushed over to the other side of the road, without even looking to see if there were any cars coming. A blonde woman was standing on the opposite pavement.

I grabbed Martha's hand in case she had any ideas about running across the road after Mum. By the time she and I had carefully crossed the road, Mum was deep in conversation with the blonde woman who was laughing away with her as if they were old friends. I didn't recognize her, even close up.

'This is Kate,' Mum told us when we caught up with her.

'Wow – is this Martha?' Kate gasped, staring at my sister excitedly. 'Sophie's just over there, Isobel. See!' She pointed at a dark-haired little girl about the same age as Martha, who was buying a pink stick of rock from a souvenir stall. The little girl came running over to us with the rock. She had long dark hair and plump rosy cheeks like Martha's.

'You won't remember, Sophie, but you two knew each other when you were babies,' Kate said, pointing out Martha, who was battling to control the drips on her ice cream. Kate glanced quickly at Mum. 'It *is* OK to mention that?'

'Oh yes! They know all about it.'

'Yes. Sophie knows too. We always thought it was best to tell her the truth.'

'Did you tell her about the mix-up?'

'The mix-up?'

'With the babies. That day.'

'You mean when . . .' Kate trailed off, shaking her head. Even I could tell she didn't want to talk about whatever it was, but Mum didn't seem to notice.

'That Mother and Baby Unit should have been closed down after that, if you ask me.'

I was listening intently now. What was Mum talking about? Was it something to do with her time in the hospital?

'Those were scary days,' Kate said hoarsely. 'I've been well since though.' She swallowed. 'What about you?'

'I'm fine!' Mum was looking at Sophie, who was showing Martha the letters on the rock she had bought. Martha was having trouble with her ice cream, which was melting so fast it was dripping on to her hand, unlike mine, which was already licked neatly down to the cone. (I can eat ice cream pretty quickly when I'm not chucking it on the ground.)

'You must be Martha's big brother,' Kate said to me while Mum kept staring in the direction of the girls. 'Your mum told me about you when we were in hospital together. You probably don't remember much about that, do you?'

I shook my head.

'You know . . . Sophie doesn't look anything like you,' Mum suddenly said loudly to Kate.

Kate looked like she thought that was an odd thing for Mum to say. 'No. She takes after her dad.' She glanced at me. '*You* look like your mum,' she said, smiling.

I nodded. People were always saying that.

'Well, we'd better go, I suppose. We're meant to be meeting my husband in a minute.' She held out her hand for her daughter. 'Come on, Sophie!' She was looking at Mum again. 'Great to see you again, Isobel. Take care!' And she waved goodbye to Martha, holding Sophie's hand tightly as they headed off together.

Mum had a funny look on her face as she kept staring after them.

'Mum, who *was* that?' I asked.

Martha started tugging at Mum's hand, whining, 'Mummy, my ice cream's all melting!'

Mum shook her off abruptly, which I would have done since Martha's hands and face were a pink sticky mess, but which Mum wouldn't normally do at all. Normally she'd be paying Martha's hands and face lots of attention just now, using up half a packet of wet wipes on them.

'Mum, who *was* that?' I said again, hearing my voice go up a pitch. I don't know why I felt so nervous all of a sudden.

'Kate was in the next bed to me in the Mother

and Baby Unit. Her baby had fair hair and mine had dark.'

'You mean the other way round, don't you?' I glanced at Martha, whose blonde hair was blowing into her ice cream.

'No,' Mum replied, looking wistful. '*My* baby had dark hair. A whole thatch of it. *Hers* was blonde, like her.'

'But, Mum—' I stopped. She had reached into her bag for a pen and she was writing something on the back of her hand. I'd never seen Mum write on her hand before. Normally she tells me off if I do it and makes me go and fetch a bit of paper. 'What are you writing?'

'Kate's holiday address here. It's a B. & B. on Castle Road. Mariner's Cottage.'

'Are you going to see her again then?' I asked, surprised. From the way Kate had whizzed away at the end of their meeting, it hadn't looked to me like she was planning on that.

Mum didn't reply. 'Come on,' she said. 'You bring Martha. We have to get home.'

On the way back I asked, 'Mum, what's a Mother and Baby Unit? Is it where people go when they've just had a baby?'

Mum looked at me. 'The one I'm talking about was in the psychiatric hospital. It's better for babies to stay with their mothers rather than be separated from them, even if their mothers have a mental illness. So some psychiatric hospitals have these special units where the babies can be looked after too.'

'But why should your one have been closed down? What was wrong with it?'

'Something happened there that shouldn't have happened. Your dad didn't think it was safe any more, so he took Martha home. Don't you remember him bringing Martha home from the hospital without me? That would have been the first time you got to see her?'

I shook my head. My memories of that time are really hazy. 'What happened?'

But she wouldn't tell me any more.

Mum and I both raced to the phone when it rang later that evening.

'Dad!' I gasped, getting there first.

'G'day, mate!' Dad was always putting on a fake Australian accent when he phoned us, which I thought was silly since he was in New Zealand.

'Dad, is Grandma—' I just stopped myself from blurting out, *Is Grandma dead yet?* Last time he'd phoned he'd told us that she had taken a turn for the worse and been admitted to hospital.

'They gave her a blood transfusion. She's back home again now.'

'Right.' I tried to sound cool about it. I knew that if Grandma died sooner than we'd expected, Dad would be able to come home sooner than we'd expected, that was all. Not that I was wishing Grandma would hurry up and die. Not really.

'Malcolm?' Mum grabbed the phone off me in her excitement to speak to him.

'Mum, can I go on the other phone?' I whispered, and she nodded. We did that quite a lot when Dad was on the line. Mum would be on the downstairs phone and Martha and I would share the upstairs extension at the same time so we could all get to speak to him at once. Martha was already in bed tonight though.

By the time I picked up the phone upstairs, Dad was telling Mum that Grandma's doctor thought she had a few weeks left to live at the most. Dad wanted to stay with her until then. 'But, Izzy, are *you* OK? I hate being away from you like this.'

'I'm fine, Malcolm.'

'And the kids? Is Daniel behaving himself?'

I nearly interrupted indignantly that of course I was, but Mum swiftly replied on my behalf. 'I told you before, Malcolm. He's being very good. A big help, in fact.' I wondered if she was going to tell him about me going to the hospital with her. Or if she'd already mentioned that when he'd phoned before.

'That's great. I thought he might be giving you a hard time about school.'

I realized then that Dad didn't know I was listening in and that Mum seemed to have forgotten. I was about to speak to let them know I was there when Dad suddenly asked, 'And you're still taking the same dose of lithium?'

'Of course.' Mum sounded a bit impatient.

I was shocked by how convincing her lie sounded. I *almost* had the courage to butt in and tell Dad the truth, but then, Mum was right about Dad worrying if he knew – and, anyway, she hadn't got ill like he'd thought she would if she ever stopped it. Besides, Mum was the parent who was here with me right now, whereas Dad was thousands of miles away. And I wasn't sure how angry Mum would be with me if I told.

'Are you managing OK with work and every-thing? You sound very . . . *perky* . . .'

'I'm fine, Malcolm. I'm just happy to hear your voice! I'm having the time of my life up at that school, bossing everyone about! I love being Head.'

He laughed. 'Are you sleeping better?'

'Yes. I told you. I'm fine. Now, what about you?'

Dad started to talk about what was happening at his end and how he was feeling about it all. I felt guilty continuing to listen in when he thought he was having a private conversation with Mum, so I decided to hang up. But just as I was about to, Mum interrupted him to say, 'You'll never guess who I met today!'

'Who?' Dad had been in the middle of telling Mum about the injections his mother was getting to ease the pain and how he had offered to give the injections himself so the nurse didn't have to visit so often. He sounded a bit surprised by Mum changing the subject so abruptly.

'Kate! Do you remember her? She was in the bed next to me on the Mother and Baby Unit. She used to come and see me on the other ward after I got moved. Anyway, she's here with her husband, taking a late summer holiday . . . *after* her daughter's school's gone back, and you know what I think about *that* . . . anyway, the little girl was with her. She's Martha's age now, of course. And, Malcolm, she has dark hair. *Dark* hair.' She paused. 'Kate had a blonde baby, remember?'

'I can't say I remember Kate very well – or her baby.'

'Well, I do, and it's made me think about it.'

'Think about *what*?' Dad sounded puzzled.

'You *know* what!'

'No I don't! Izzy, what are you saying?'

'I'm not saying anything!' Mum snapped. 'It was just a shock seeing them, that's all. It brought it all back! It's all right for you! You weren't the one who had your baby taken away from you, were you?'

'Izzy . . .' he began, sounding concerned, then he broke off. There were other voices in the background and Dad's name was being called. 'Izzy, the nurse is here to see my mother. I have to go, but we'll talk properly later, OK?' He paused. 'Izzy, I'm sorry . . . I'm sorry you're upset . . . You are OK, aren't you?'

'Of course I am. I'm just really missing you, that's all. And then this happened . . .'

'I'm missing you too, love.'

I wanted to put the phone down in case they started to get slushy, but I was worried that they would hear it, so I forced myself to wait until they'd hung up.

I was having difficulty making sense of what I'd just heard. All that stuff about Martha. Had something happened back then that nobody had told me? I had only been four or five and I couldn't remember what Mum had been like when she got ill. Dad had sent me to stay with Uncle Robert and Aunt Sandra when it all started. That had been before they split up and Aunt Sandra moved back to Scotland. I think Dad looked after me on his own for a while after Mum went in to hospital. I do remember Dad coming home one day and telling me I had a new baby sister. And I remember a nanny coming and living in our spare room for a while. She hadn't stayed long. I think maybe she and Dad didn't get on all that well. I tried to remember the day Dad had brought Martha home but I couldn't. And the only colour I can ever remember her hair being is the colour it is now.

8

Mum didn't say anything else about the woman called Kate – or her daughter – for the rest of the week, and I thought it was best not to ask. She had organized for a local removal firm to take our two sofas up to the school in time for the book sale on Saturday morning. That was enough to worry about for one week, I reckoned. I'd tried to talk her out of it but she wouldn't listen. She said that as Head Teacher she had a duty to set an example to the rest of the school by donating our furniture.

When we got to the school ourselves on Saturday, our sofas were the only ones there. They looked really silly sitting on their own in the middle of the assembly hall. Martha immediately ran over and curled up on one of them and a parent who was helping out gushed, 'Oh, isn't she a cutie? You'd better watch someone doesn't try and buy *her* today! Look at that lovely blonde hair! Where does she get that from?'

Mum looked at Martha. 'Not from anybody in *our* family,' she said, and walked away abruptly. I thought that was a really weird thing to say.

Mrs Lyle was busy setting up the book stalls when we arrived. As soon as she saw Mum she came over and explained that since we only had the two sofas she'd thought we should have stalls after all. But she was also going to set up a sort of cosy corner with our sofas, so that people could relax there when they wanted to have a break from book-hunting. There was a plant stall, I noticed, although there weren't very many plants on it. Mum spotted that too. 'I'm going home to fetch some more things,' she said. 'I won't be long.'

'What things?' I asked, but she didn't reply.

She came back half an hour later carrying Dad's massive cheese plant.

'But, Mum, Dad likes that plant!' I gasped. 'He's had it since he was a medical student!'

'Yes, and if I don't get rid of it, he'll have it until he's an old-age pensioner,' Mum replied.

'But, Mum, he won't want you to get rid of it.'

Mum just ignored me. She's not very good with plants. She says the big ones take up too much room and block out the light and the little ones make her feel like a failure because they're always going brown and dying on her. She'd already thrown one in the bin the day after Dad left. (It still had one green leaf, which Dad had insisted was a good enough reason to keep it.) I could understand Mum wanting to throw out that one, but I still couldn't believe she was going to sell his precious cheese plant without telling him.

It turned out Mum wasn't just selling the cheese plant. She had loaded all our house plants into the car and now she was bringing them into the hall one by one. 'Mum, you can't do this!' I gasped as I watched her place Dad's favourite cactus plant –

which sprouted pink flowers in the winter – on the table.

'I can do anything!' she grinned. 'I'm the head, aren't I?'

She went over to the home-made-cake stall next. That looked like the part of Mum's idea that had really caught on. Lots of people had brought stuff for it. Mum had bought six jam-and-cream sponges from Tesco and got me and Martha to ice them last night and now she was telling everyone that my sister and I had been up all night baking them. It was going to be really embarrassing if we got found out, and I just hoped Martha wasn't going to open her mouth and give the game away.

Mum had this other idea for the cake stall too, which wasn't anything to do with cakes. She'd bought a whole load of eggs and left some of them whole and broken the others and emptied out the insides. She'd put the upturned empty eggshells back in the box with the whole eggs and people had to pay to have a go at choosing one. If they picked a whole egg instead of an eggshell they got the egg and a rasher of bacon to go with it. She'd got the idea because it was something they'd done at the Christmas fair when *she* was at school.

'Mrs MacKenzie, I really don't think we can do that,' Mrs Lyle said, looking worried when Mum pulled the packets of bacon out of her bag and started to rip them open. 'There are food hygiene regulations for things like this. We don't want to give people food poisoning and get the school into trouble.'

'Yes, Mum – people might die!' I blurted out,

eager to back up Mrs Lyle, because I thought it was a crazy idea too.

Mrs Lyle flushed. '*Of course,* if people were to die that would be more important than the school being in trouble,' she said, as if she thought I was implying that she valued the reputation of the school above human life.

I flushed too. I hadn't meant it like that. I'd only been trying to help. Trust Mrs Lyle to take it the wrong way. But I couldn't think of anything to say to make it clear that I hadn't been having a dig at her and, anyway, at least Mum was taking the eggs off the stall.

At ten o'clock Mrs Lyle opened the doors and people started to come in.

Mum stood behind the cake stall for a while, then she said her main role as Head Teacher was to mingle. She told me that while she was mingling she was going to distribute some leaflets she'd made and she wanted me to do the same. She gave me a bundle to hand out and disappeared off to speak to the parent who had just purchased Dad's favourite cactus.

My stomach flipped over when I saw what was on the leaflets. DO YOU WANT TO CHANGE OUR SCHOOL UNIFORM? it said. IF SO, PLEASE TICK PREFERRED COLOURS. There were boxes for GREEN, PURPLE, RED, ORANGE, YELLOW and BLUE (*NOT* NAVY).

I stared at my mother, who was wearing a red dress with a bright orange cardigan over it, which actually looked quite nice in a traffic-lightish sort of way. Was this a joke? Apparently not, because she was handing out leaflets to everyone within arm's length and also trying to stick one to the front of the nearest book stall.

'HEY! DANIEL!'

I looked up. Abby was heading towards me. A young woman with short dark hair was with her. When Mrs Lyle saw her she rushed over 'Susie, you've come back to visit us! How lovely!' she exclaimed.

'That's my big sister,' Abby explained. 'She was sort of like Mrs Lyle's pet, though she goes mad if you say that to her!' She looked at the leaflets in my hand. 'What are you doing?'

'Mum told me to give these out.'

'Let's see.' She took one from me. 'Wow! Is she *serious*? I'm going to show this to Susie. She'll think it's a hoot.'

'Abby – *wait*!' I put out my hand to stop her from taking the leaflet over to her sister, who was still deep in conversation with Mrs Lyle. As far as I could tell, Mrs Lyle hadn't actually seen one of Mum's leaflets yet.

Abby looked at me expectantly.

'So does your sister still live at home then?' I blurted out. It was the first thing I could think of to say to keep her there.

'Susie's the *only* one at home,' Abby answered. 'Dad's up north somewhere. We never see him.' She kept looking at me steadily, as if she was testing me in some sort of way. 'My mum lives in her own place. I used to live with her but it didn't work out, so now I live with Susie.'

'Right.' I didn't know what else to say. I hadn't

81

expected my question to generate quite that much information. I felt like I ought to make a suitable response only I couldn't think of one. 'Umm . . . Do you want a cheese scone?' I shoved the plate under her nose. They had been baked by Mrs Lyle and they looked like the best thing on the stall, chiefly because they didn't have hideous pink icing on them like all the things Mum had donated.

Abby picked up the biggest one. 'You buying?'

'Sure.' I dropped enough money for two into the margarine tub we were using to collect the cash.

Abby grinned suddenly, looking across at Mrs Lyle's cosy corner. 'I can't believe your mum really brought in your sofas.'

'I know,' I muttered gloomily.

'And I can't believe she's really thinking of changing the colour of our school uniform! I mean, is that wacky or what?'

'Listen, Abby,' I said, feeling irritated. 'Shut up about my mum, OK?'

She looked at me in surprise. I thought she might be going to say something snappish back, which I guess I deserved, but she didn't. She just said, 'OK, mate,' and gave me a sympathetic smile, as if feeling embarrassed by your mother was something she understood only too well.

Mum was in a bad mood with me in the car on the way home and not just because I kept playing with the buttons that make the electric windows go up and down. She was cross because I had bought Dad's cheese plant back and only told her when the sale was over that the RESERVED sticker attached to one of its leaves meant it was reserved for *us*. Mum had refused to let me bring it home with us and said it could stay in the corner of the school hall, where hopefully it would die from lack of water. I didn't tell her that I'd asked our school caretaker if he would water it until Dad got the chance to fetch it back.

As soon as we got home, Martha ran over to feed her goldfish and let out a scream. One of the fish – the one with the white spot on its side – was floating on the surface, obviously dead.

'Look!' Mum pointed at a fish who was taking a bite out of the dead one. 'You should have called that one Jaws!' She banged on the side of the tank with her fist. 'Hey, it's Hannibal the Cannibal!'

'Mum, Martha's really upset!' I hissed.

'Oh, baby!' Mum crooned. 'Don't be upset. We'll have a funeral. A proper fishy funeral. It'll be fun! No flushing down the loo for this fish! Daniel, you fish out the fish. I'll fetch a coffin.' She whizzed off into the kitchen.

'It's R-Rupert,' Martha sobbed as I used the little fishing net we'd bought from the pet shop to scoop out the little orange body. 'He was my f-favourite.'

'Da-dah!' Mum boomed, like she was a magician at a kiddies' party instead of a mother in charge of a sobbing little girl who had just lost her favourite fish. I couldn't believe she was behaving like this. It was as if she didn't have any idea how Martha was feeling at all. 'One fishy coffin!' She rammed Rupert into the matchbox she'd just emptied as I tried to comfort my sister. 'We'll give him a funeral to die for!' Mum started laughing. 'A funeral to die for! Get it?' She grabbed Martha's hand and pulled her towards the door. 'We'll bury him at sea – just like they bury sailors!'

'But Rupert's *not* a sailor,' Martha sniffed, trying to twist her hand free from Mum's.

'No – he's a floater!' Mum dropped Martha's hand to do an impersonation of a dead fish with two sticky-out fins and staring eyes.

I tried to keep a straight face, because I thought it was a really sick joke, but I have got to admit that it was difficult. As dead-fish impressions go, Mum's was pretty funny.

Mum and I had a huge row the following day. Mum accused me of being a stick-in-the-mud and too big for my boots. I told her she was a rotten mother. I ended up getting sent to my room, which I didn't care about. I was just glad to get away from her.

The thing that started the row was me having a go at Mum – again – about how she'd gone swimming in the sea in her bra and knickers after we'd thrown Rupert off the end of the pier the day before. Mum told me I was a prude and that if she wanted to go swimming in the nude then she'd do that too. I couldn't believe it when she said that. Normally she gets self-conscious even lying in a swimsuit on the beach, and she won't wear a bikini because she says it shows too much of her fat tummy. Mum was acting differently to how she'd ever acted before and I didn't know if it was because Dad wasn't around or because she was a headmistress now or – and this was the thought that worried me the most – because she'd stopped taking her lithium tablets.

Dad had said that when Mum had stopped taking her lithium before, she had become really ill, really quickly. I'd been trying to remember what Mum was like when she was ill but I couldn't. I tried to imagine what a person would be like if they were ill in a mental sort of way, but the only mentally ill people I'd seen were on television. That man in *Neighbours* who had put the bomb in the coffee shop had turned out to be stark raving mad in the next episode. He'd started shouting that he was the Chosen One and that he'd heard the voice of God telling him to blow everybody up and that was why he had done it. And then he'd started running around the hospital with no clothes on. Mum certainly wasn't anything like him.

I decided to phone Dad that night when Martha was in bed and Mum was in the bathroom. I had to talk to him. If Mum was feeling stressed because Dad wasn't here then maybe if I told that to Dad, he'd try and come home a bit sooner.

It was my aunt who picked it up. It would be nine o'clock in the morning over there. 'Oh . . . Daniel. Your father can't come to the phone right now. He's helping our mother choose the hymns for her funeral.' She sounded tired.

'Can you ask him to phone us as soon as he's done?' I asked. 'It's really important.'

Aunt Helen coughed, like she'd just swallowed something that had stuck in her throat. 'You did hear what I said, didn't you? Malcolm is choosing the hymns for our mother's *funeral*? I think he might be just a little upset and not up to a big phone conversation when he's *done*, don't you?'

I realized I wasn't being very tactful, but I just really needed to speak to Dad. 'Yes, but I think Mum's really . . . really *missing* him. I think maybe he should come home sooner.'

There was a long silence at the other end. My aunt sounded upset and angry when she finally spoke. 'And *I* think this might be a time when Malcolm should put his family first.' She slammed the phone down before I could agree with her that that was what I thought too.

It was a few minutes later when I registered that by *his* family she'd meant them and not us.

I decided I'd wait and phone again tomorrow.

Mum had finished in the bathroom and now she was crashing about in the spare room where there were still lots of boxes that we hadn't unpacked. I went to see what she was doing.

She stared at me, looking up from a cardboard box she had just opened. 'I can't find the photos.'

'What photos?'

'The photos of Martha. *My* Martha. In the hospital.'

'Do you want me to help you look?'

We carried on searching together, and eventually she came across the box she was looking for. Shoved at the back of an old photo album were some baby photographs of Martha that I'd never seen before.

'Your dad doesn't like seeing these pictures,' Mum told me. He says it reminds him of a time he'd rather forget. But that's not the real reason he won't look at them.'

'What *is* the real reason?' I asked, curious.

Mum didn't reply. She was peering closely at a picture of herself holding Martha in her arms.

I stared at the picture. I had never seen it before. It was a really bad photo of Mum. She was sitting up in bed in hospital, wearing a pink night-dress, and her dark hair was all over the place. It was her face that was the most disturbing though. She had this really fixed grin and her eyes were star-ing at the camera in a frenzied sort of way, wide open with too much of the whites of her eyes show-ing. She looked just like you'd ask an actress to look if they were playing the part of a mad woman in a horror movie. No wonder Dad had never wanted anyone to see it. She was clutching a tiny baby in her arms tightly, as if she were afraid it was going to squirm away from her if she let go. The baby was wrapped in a blanket and the cover had been pulled over its head like a hood. It looked all tiny and wrinkly. I couldn't take my eyes off the mother in the picture though. I mean, I knew that was Mum, but somehow I couldn't *feel* as if it was. I picked up the other photographs that had been taken at the same time and thankfully she looked pretty normal in those, apart from looking tired and not smiling at all. There was a photo of her and the woman called Kate both standing with their babies. The babies were wearing identical pink knitted bonnets and matching cardigans and they looked like twins.

'*This* is my baby!' Mum said, pointing at the baby in her arms in the picture.

I nodded. 'That's Martha, right?'

'*My* baby had dark hair.'

'You can't see her hair,' I pointed out.

'I don't have to see it to remember it!' She turned to look at me. 'I'm not saying they did it on purpose. But after it happened, nobody would admit it. They're like that, these doctors. They all close ranks.'

'After *what* happened?' I frowned. 'What are you talking about, Mum?'

Mum suddenly seemed angry. 'They thought I was too mad to know my own baby! That's what they thought!'

I took a step back from her. What was wrong with her? She wasn't making any sense.

We heard the door creak and Martha was standing in the doorway. Her face was screwed up and she was rubbing at her eyes. She saw the photographs Mum was holding and came over to look at them. She giggled when she saw the really bad picture of Mum. 'You look funny, Mummy.' Then she pointed at the baby. 'Is that me?'

'No,' Mum said. 'It's not!'

I stared at her. 'But I thought you just said—'

'Who is it then?' Martha asked, reaching up to smooth down Mum's hair. Martha is always trying to tidy Mum's hair. 'Is it Daniel?'

Mum didn't reply. She was starting to cry silently. 'Go away,' she whispered, in a choked voice, pushing Martha away from her.

Martha looked shocked and screwed up her face as if she was about to start crying too.

I felt scared then, though I wasn't really sure why.

88

I took Martha back to her room and, as I kissed her goodnight, her bottom lip trembled as she asked, 'What's wrong with Mummy?'

'Nothing,' I said hoarsely. 'She's just missing Daddy.' And I turned off the light.

I phoned Dad again as soon as I'd left her room but this time the phone was engaged. I tried a few times but it kept on sounding the same. Maybe my aunt had deliberately taken it off the hook.

9

First thing the next morning Dad phoned us. He was phoning from the hospital. Grandma had taken a turn for the worse and had been rushed into hospital a few hours ago. Dad said she wasn't going to have a blood transfusion this time because there wasn't any point.

Mum had picked up the phone first and I stood by, listening as he told all of this to her. She kept saying, 'I'm sorry, darling,' over and over. She looked a bit dazed and, when she'd finished speaking to him, she put the phone down straight away instead of handing it over to me.

'I wanted to speak to him,' I said.

'Later, Daniel. You can't just now. Your grandmother sounds like she's fading fast.'

It wasn't that I didn't care about what was happening to my grandmother, but I had other things I needed to ask Mum about since I obviously couldn't ask Dad now. 'Mum . . . what you said last night—' I began, but I had to stop as Martha came running into the room to remind us that if we didn't hurry up we'd all be late for school.

I waited until we'd dropped Martha off before tackling Mum again. (I was letting her give me a lift to school too today because we were running so late.) 'Mum, what did you mean last night about that baby not being Martha?' I asked.

Mum turned to look at me. 'Listen, Daniel . . .' She seemed suddenly distracted by my school tie. Her eyes lit up as she started to tell me her latest idea for our new school uniform. She was going to commission the same dressmaker who had made many of Princess Diana's clothes to design it for her.

'But, Mum, what about—'

'Red is a much better colour for a school than grey!' she interrupted. 'We'll change everything grey to red! Pillar-box red or strawberry red? What do you think?'

'Mum, stop it!'

'Stop what?'

'Stop acting like . . . like you did with the book sale! Stop acting like your ideas are more important than everybody else's!'

She laughed. 'They *are* more important! I'm the head!'

'But, Mum, it's not like the school *belongs* to you!' I protested. 'I mean, what about all the other teachers? What about what *they* think?'

'Daniel,' she laughed again. 'You are so serious! So like your dad . . . always worrying!' And she planted a big kiss on my cheek even though I'd have rather she'd just kept facing straight ahead since she was driving round a roundabout at the time.

We were almost at the school, so I made her stop the car to let me out before anyone saw us together. I would have to wait until this evening to ask her what she'd meant about Martha not being the baby in those photographs. But I was going to ask her just the same.

In assembly, I sat there keeping much more still than I normally do, wishing I could sink through the floor and disappear, because Mum was wearing her most hideous skirt-and-cardigan combination yet. She beamed at everyone as she announced that red was going to be our new school colour from now on. She wanted everyone to wear a red jumper or cardigan to school tomorrow and if they didn't have one they had to wear a red scarf or something else red instead. A ripple of murmurs went round the hall and I could see the teachers staring at each other as if they couldn't believe what they were hearing.

'The morale in a school is very important,' Mum continued rapidly. 'And this *greyness* is enough to depress anyone.'

The whole hall was muttering noisily now. I wanted to crawl under my chair and stay there until assembly had finished. Any minute now someone was going to remember that the weirdo head teacher was my mother.

In science everyone was talking about Mum, but amazingly they weren't saying horrible things. They kept saying she was *cool* or *wicked* as they discussed what red thing they were going to wear to school the next day. I started to swing my feet backwards and forwards impatiently. I wished our teacher, Mr Davie, would hurry up and get there before it dawned on anyone that what Mum was doing was actually pretty strange. Thankfully Calum wasn't in my science class or I reckon he'd already have been having a go at me.

When Mr Davie hadn't arrived ten minutes into the lesson, the noise level started to get pretty deafening. Mr Gregory, the head of science, came into the room, scowling at us. 'Mr Davie seems to have mysteriously absented himself since assembly, so I have no option but to take the class instead,' he grunted. 'Get out your books, please.'

We all stifled groans. Mr Gregory is a scruffy little man with popping-out eyes, and I'd never liked him ever since Mum had made that comment about him staring at her legs. Science was usually fun with Mr Davie, who was always just as keen as we were to get the boring stuff over with so we could get on with our attempts to blow up the lab (which was how he always referred to our experiments). Mr Gregory seemed to be spending all his time going over the theory and it looked like we were going to be lucky if we got anywhere near an empty test tube today, let alone a Bunsen burner.

The room was hot and my head, which I was resting on my hands, felt really muzzy. Before I knew it my head had slumped on to my desk and I couldn't hear Mr Gregory's drony voice any more. I don't know how long I'd been like that before Mr Gregory came over and poked me in the arm.

'You!' he snapped. 'Go outside and get some fresh air! You can come back when you've woken up again!'

A few of the other kids started to snigger as I stood up and headed groggily towards the door. I felt dizzy, as if all the blood was rushing back to my head at once.

I was just heading down the corridor towards the

staircase when I saw someone hurrying towards me from the far end. The person was wearing a bright red skirt and a yellow cardigan.

'Daniel!' It was Mum. 'Daniel, it *is* you!' She started to laugh in a delighted sort of way, as if she hadn't seen me in several years instead of just this morning. She didn't ask why I wasn't in class. 'I'm touring my school,' she announced grandly. 'I want to see what all my subjects are doing.'

'Subjects?' I queried, thinking that she had to be joking. I mean, a queen has subjects, right, not a headmistress?

'Science, English, history, French, maths . . . Loyal subjects, to name but a few!' Mum rattled on. 'Oh, and I've locked that Davie man in the book cupboard with that French student. That'll teach the two of them to sneak in there for a snog when they should be working!'

I stared at her. I thought she was joking at first. Then I saw she had a strange look in her eyes – a shiny, whizzy sort of look as if she was up in the sky like a firework.

10

I heard the pounding on the door before I got to the book cupboard. The book cupboard in the languages department is one of those big walk-in ones, more like a mini room than a cupboard really, except that there are no windows. It's situated at the end of the corridor on the far side of the toilets and the language lab is the nearest classroom along the corridor. Everyone in the lab probably had their headphones on and couldn't hear the banging. I didn't know what I was going to say when I unlocked the door. I just knew that I had to unlock it quickly before Mum got into trouble. She had laughed when I'd said what I was going to do, and headed off towards her own office on the floor below rather than coming with me.

I unlocked the door and Mr Davie almost fell out. Yvette, our French student teacher, was right behind him.

'Daniel, thank goodness!' Mr Davie looked a mixture of relieved and embarrassed. 'Yvette and I were just . . .' He went pink. 'Collecting some textbooks when . . . someone locked the door. They must have thought there was nobody inside.'

'*Someone?*' I repeated, trying not to sound as nervous as I felt. 'Didn't you see who?'

'No.'

'*I* think it was one of the girls having a joke,' Yvette said. 'We heard a silly laugh outside.'

'Do you think you'll be able to find out who it was?' I asked, trying to sound casual about it, which wasn't how I felt at all.

The two teachers were looking at each other.

'I think we will not make a fuss, Stephen – I mean, Mister Davie . . .' Yvette said. 'Since it was just a joke, no?'

Mr Davie nodded. 'I agree. No point in making a fuss. I'd better get back to my class now.' He looked at me. 'Daniel . . .'

I started to see that they were both just as anxious as I was that nobody else should find out about this. I began to feel more hopeful. 'I won't tell anyone either,' I said. 'If it means no one's going to get into trouble for shutting you in. None of the other kids, I mean,' I added quickly.

Mr Davie was staring at me now. 'You don't *know* who shut us in here, do you, Daniel?'

I gulped. 'Of course not! Mr Gregory's taking our class,' I added. 'He sent me out for some fresh air because I fell asleep. I'd better hurry up.'

Mr Davie called after me as I ran away down the corridor, 'See you back in the classroom in ten minutes, OK?'

'OK!' I shouted back to him.

I went to find Mum in her office. Her door was open and her secretary wasn't there. I could hear her on the phone to someone. 'What do you mean, you can't give me their address? I'm an old friend. And I'm a head teacher. I need to contact them urgently.' She listened for a few moments longer, then slammed down the phone.

'Mum . . .' I paused nervously just inside the doorway. I lowered my voice. 'I let Mr Davie and Yvette out of the book cupboard. They don't know it was you who shut them in. I thought we'd better not tell them. It'll be really embarrassing if anyone finds out.'

Mum ignored me like she'd forgotten all about that now. 'They won't give me Kate's address!' she said angrily.

'Who won't?'

'That B. & B. where she was staying.' Mum was drumming her fingers on the desk. 'How can I find her? I must find her!'

'Mum, why do you need to find Kate? Is it about Martha? Is it about what happened when Martha was a baby?'

I'd thought I'd have to beg her to tell me. But I was wrong. She blurted it all out right there in her office. 'It happened when she was a few days old, Daniel. Only a mother can recognize her own baby when it's that tiny. That's why I'm the only one who knows.'

'Knows *what*, Mum?'

'That she was swapped!' She had that extra-bright look in her eyes again.

'*Swapped!*' I spluttered.

Mum started to speak in short, fast bursts. 'I got home. I knew she was a different baby. He told me I was mad to think it.'

I couldn't believe what she was saying. I mean, she *couldn't* really think that. 'Mum, that can't be right! Martha *couldn't* have been swapped for another baby!'

'There was a patient who thought the babies were hers. All of them. All the babies,' Mum continued. 'She took some of them off the ward. She took mine. And Kate's.' Mum shuddered. 'They got them back but it must have happened then. I didn't see Martha again after that. Malcolm was frightened. He took her away. Home with him. It was too late by the time I found out.'

'Mum, stop it!' I shouted angrily. I couldn't bear to hear this. Mum was talking nonsense. Dad wouldn't have just let Martha be swapped for another baby like that.

'I could tell Kate knew the truth!' Mum continued. 'She knew but she wanted *my* baby.'

'Mum, stop it!' I shouted again. 'Why would Kate want your baby? That's just stupid!'

'Because she's a royal baby!' Mum shouted back. 'That's why!'

I just gaped at her. Now, she wasn't making any sense at all.

I persuaded Mum to go home straight away. I thought I should go with her because she was so upset, but Mum wouldn't listen to me. She insisted I stay in school and when I tried to refuse she started to shout at me again. I was scared other people would hear us if I didn't give in, so we agreed I'd see her later at home. She left a note for her secretary saying she wasn't feeling well and slipped away while everyone else was still in class. I was so relieved to get her off the premises that I didn't even think that she might not really be going home like she'd said. When I got home I was going to call Dad and ask him what to do. Hopefully my grandmother would have died by now and he'd be able to come home straight away.

I couldn't believe I was thinking that thought – that Grandma would hurry up and die. It was like my world had just flipped upside down and all the normal things in it had become abnormal. I went around the school for the rest of the day in a weird kind of daze, like I was a visitor from another planet, rather than a normal person who was actually part of life on planet Earth.

When I got home after school the house was empty, but there was a message on the answerphone from Mum. She said she was going to London, because she had got hold of Kate's address after all.

I phoned her on her mobile straight away. She was in the car.

'Mum, what are you doing? You can't drive to London!'

'Of course I can. I'm halfway there now! I went to the B. & B. – there was a young girl there helping out. I got Kate's address from her. I'm going to see her now.'

'But Mum—'

She had hung up.

I phoned her back. I was really worried now.

'Mum, are you *feeling* OK?' I asked when she answered. I meant, was she feeling OK *mentally*?

'Of course!'

'You don't seem . . . *normal*.'

She laughed. 'I'm full of energy, Daniel. I've been a zombie for years on those tablets. For years I've been tranquillized on those things. Now I'm feeling everything at last!'

I felt confused. Was she right? *Was* this normal? She didn't seem very normal but then what was normal exactly?

'Must go, darling.' And she hung up again. I didn't ring back this time. She hasn't got a hands-free phone and I didn't want her having an accident because she was using her mobile while she was driving. (Mum's the one who's always telling us how dangerous it is to drive and do anything else at the same time – like use your mobile, or unwrap a sweet or fiddle with the radio like Dad does a lot.)

If only Dad was here now. I rang my aunt's number to see if they were home from the hospital yet but there was no reply. Then I remembered it would only be about four o'clock in the morning over there, so even if they were home, they might all be asleep.

I didn't know what to do. It just wasn't like Mum not to care that Martha needed collecting from her after-school club or that our tea needed making or that I had asked her to take me to the library tonight. It was like she had forgotten all about Martha and me. And I couldn't believe what she had said about Martha not being the right baby. She had never said anything like that before. And all that stuff she had said about *Kate* having her baby . . .

Mum must have got it wrong. She *must* have. I mean, babies being accidently swapped in hospital and getting sent home with the wrong parents . . . that stuff only ever happens in films, right? Or maybe occasionally in real life in places where they make babies out of test tubes a lot. And what had Mum meant about Kate knowing about it and wanting to keep Martha because she was *royal*?

I kept turning everything over in my head as I walked to Martha's school to collect her, but I still couldn't make any sense out of it.

As soon as she saw me, Martha wanted to know where Mum was, so I told her she had gone to London but she'd be back tonight.

'But there has to be a grown-up to look after us.' Martha frowned.

'I'll look after you,' I said. 'It'll be cool. It'll be like in that movie we saw at Uncle Robert's, *Home Alone*!'

Too late I remembered that Martha had got scared watching *Home Alone* and had to be taken out of the room by Mum when the bit with the nasty burglars came on. Her face crumpled. 'I don't want you to look after me. I want Mummy.'

'Well, Mummy's not here. And even if she was—' I stopped myself just in time. I'd been about to say that even if she *was* here, the way Mum was acting right now, she'd be more likely to *invite* scary burglars into our house rather than protect us from them.

On the walk home we had to pass the park and Martha begged to have a go on the swings, so I said OK.

'Hey!' someone shouted to me. It was Abby. She had a friend with her – nobody I recognized from school.

'Hi,' I said, walking up to them.

Abby's friend was saying, 'I can't come back with you, Abby – I've got to get home.' She had short red hair and a freckled face and she was wearing shorts and an England football shirt.

Abby turned and smiled at me. 'Hiya.' She turned back to her friend who was looking me over now. 'This is Daniel. He sits next to me at school. He's just moved here and his mum's our head teacher.'

'*Really?*' Abby's friend looked like she found that horrific. 'Poor you.'

I nodded, flushing slightly. 'Yeah,' I agreed.

Abby laughed. 'This is Rachel. She's being really boring and going home now so she's not late for her tea.' She looked at me. 'But you can hang around with me for a bit, can't you?'

'Not really,' I said. 'I've got to look after my little sister. Mum's gone out.'

Abby didn't seem phased. 'No problem. We can all hang out together.'

I still wasn't sure. I mean, what if Dad phoned? But on the other hand, Dad wasn't likely to phone since it was still night-time in New Zealand.

Rachel said, 'See you later. Michael says he's gonna get you back for the other day, by the way.'

'Fat chance!' Abby grinned, waving her friend goodbye. 'Michael's her twin brother,' she said to me. 'I beat him scoring goals the other week. He's a rubbish goalie.'

'You play *football*?'

She nodded. 'Why? Didn't you think girls could kick a ball?'

I flushed. 'No, it's just—'

'I'm better than Michael, though he won't admit that. Do you play?'

I nodded. 'I used to play all the time back home . . . I mean back where I used to live.'

'Michael and his friends and Rachel and me all play down the park most Saturdays. You can come too if you want.'

'Great!' I grinned, momentarily forgetting about everything else. Football down the park sounded like the best thing that had happened to me since I got here.

Abby and I sat on the swings while Martha ran about climbing on one thing after another. Normally in parks I climb on stuff too and chase Martha about, but since Abby was chatting to me I reckoned it would be rude not to stay put and listen. I tried to stop thinking about Mum, but it was difficult. I suddenly really wanted to ask someone else what *they* thought about the way she was acting.

Abby asked where I lived and when I told her she offered to call in for me on her way to school.

'OK,' I said, watching her bend down to pick up a sweet she'd just dropped on the ground. 'Abby—'

But I was interrupted by my sister. 'You can't eat that!' Martha shouted in her bossiest voice, from the top of the slide. 'Daddy says the ground is full of germs!'

'Well, my sister Susie says eating stuff off the floor builds up your *resistance* to germs!' Abby

103

shouted back at her. She grinned sideways at me. 'She says that every time she drops our dinner on the floor, anyway!'

I laughed, but I realized it was going to be difficult telling Abby about Mum while Martha was within earshot. 'Abby,' I began again. 'There's something I want to tell you, but not here.' I glanced across at Martha who had slid down to the bottom of the slide and was heading back towards us. 'Can you keep a secret? Martha musn't know, OK?'

Abby grinned. I could tell she liked secrets. 'Of course. Why don't you come round to mine for a bit? Martha can watch a video in the front room and we can talk in the kitchen. We can get something to eat as well. I'm starving.'

I wasn't so sure about that. 'But what about your big sister?' I wasn't ready to let another grown-up in on all of this just yet.

'She's still at work. Anyway, she won't mind you coming round.'

'Are you sure?'

She nodded impatiently, and when Martha came over to tell us that she wanted to go home for tea now, Abby told her that we were all going to her house for tea instead.

Abby lived on the ground floor in a block of flats. They had a little garden at the back with a whirligig to hang out your washing. Abby didn't know what a whirligig was when I pointed it out. She called it a rotating clothes line. We started telling each other what we called other things then, since it turned out we had quite a few different names for stuff.

Martha kept running in and out of the kitchen

while Abby and I were making the crisp and tomato ketchup sandwiches we'd decided on for tea, but I figured once she was settled in front of the TV with her food in front of her, I'd be able to talk to Abby without her overhearing. Though I wasn't sure exactly what I was going to say yet.

Abby suddenly started telling me about her mother almost as if she knew that I was trying to get up the courage to tell her something major about mine. 'Last week she went into a special clinic to get some help to stop drinking. Susie says we musn't get our hopes up because she's done that before . . . but at least she's *trying* again.'

'That must be the hardest part,' I murmured. 'Not to get your hopes up, I mean.'

She gave me a funny look, as if she didn't know too many people who understood that. 'Here!' She put the lid back on the ketchup bottle. 'Catch!' She threw it to me across the table.

Unfortunately, I've never been brilliant at catching things.

Just as the glass bottle missed my hand and landed with a smash on the tiled floor, Abby's big sister walked in the back door. She was wearing a black duffle coat and she had a bag of shopping in her hand. 'What the hell's going on?'

'Sorry,' I gulped.

Susie was glowering at the broken bottle which was now leaking ketchup. She glared at Abby who looked like she was trying not to giggle. 'Are you just going to stand there, miss?'

Abby hurried to the sink to fetch a cloth just as Martha walked in from the living room.

'Yikes!' Susie nearly jumped out of her skin. 'What is this? Nursery school?'

'She's my sister,' I said quickly. 'We were just leaving.'

'No they weren't,' Abby said as she took a cloth over to clean up the mess. 'They can stay for tea, can't they, Susie?'

But Susie was heading towards her sister now, who was absent-mindedly swishing the cloth about the floor. 'Watch you don't cut yourself on that glass! I don't want blood everywhere as well!' She crouched down in order to deal with the broken bottle herself.

'Come on, Martha. Let's go,' I whispered. I didn't reckon I'd get a chance to talk to Abby about Mum now anyway.

'Was that Abby's mum?' Martha asked me when we were outside.

'It's her big sister.'

'She *acted* like her mum,' Martha said.

'Well, she has to look after her. That's why.'

'Why does she have to look after her?'

'Because Abby's mum and dad aren't around, OK?' I grabbed hold of her hand as we approached the main road.

'Would *you* have to look after *me*, if *our* mum and dad weren't around?' Martha asked.

'Stop asking so many questions, OK?' I said crossly, because it was giving me butterflies in my tummy, the way her gaze was fixed on me so trustingly.

11

Mum wasn't back when we got home – not that I'd really expected her to be. She wasn't even answering her mobile, though it was ringing out. Dad hadn't phoned back either. I knew it was still the early hours in New Zealand, but I thought Dad might be up and I really needed to speak to him. If only Dad had a mobile with him, or I had the number of the hospital or something. When it was time for Martha to go to bed and Mum still hadn't come home, I said, 'She'll be back when you wake up tomorrow morning. I'll read you a story to send you to sleep.' I read her this book she likes about a mermaid who finds out she's a princess. It took ages to read all of it, but I didn't want to stop because I didn't want to have to go downstairs on my own to wait for Mum.

I also didn't want to be on my own thinking about what Mum might be doing right now. What if she went and accused Kate of stealing her baby? And what if she demanded they be swapped back? Everyone would think Mum was mad, especially because she had been in a mental hospital before. But Mum couldn't be mad, could she? Even if she had got it wrong about Martha, that didn't make her mad. I didn't know exactly what a proper mad person looked like, but I reckoned they'd be talking to themselves like that man in *Neighbours* and maybe foaming at the mouth a bit and . . . I don't know . . . going around trying to take bites out of cats or something. I reckoned they'd be pretty scary and easy to spot in any case.

I lay on the sofa watching TV until really late, jumping up every time I heard a car outside. I started to worry that Mum had been involved in an accident. I didn't know how soon the police came and told you if your relative was in a car crash. My stomach was churning and every time I heard a car drive into our street I jumped up to look out of the window. Our parents had never left us alone like this before.

At midnight I heard a car outside and, when I went to look, it was Mum. I opened the front door as she tottered down the drive trailing her coat and carrying several shopping bags. 'Mum, I've been so worried,' I burst out, starting to cry, which was really stupid, but I was just so relieved that she was safe. She was wearing high heels. She hardly ever wears shoes with high heels.

'Hi, baby.' Her voice sounded funny. She came inside the house and dropped all her bags noisily on the wooden floor in the hall. She kicked off her shoes which clattered against the wall, and slammed the front door shut behind her. She didn't ask how I was or how Martha was or whether Dad had phoned. She didn't explain or say sorry about leaving us for so long. 'Sleepy,' she grinned, and started to laugh. She flopped down on the settee and closed her eyes.

I stared at her, feeling a whole mixture of things that I couldn't put into words. Like screaming. Like running away. Like holding her tight and never letting her go. Like hitting her.

I walked across to the sofa. 'Did you go to Kate's house? What did she say?'

But she didn't open her eyes. She grunted and turned over so that her face was squashed against the back of the sofa. I shook her to wake her up again but it didn't work. She seemed to have fallen asleep.

I went upstairs and into Martha's room. I didn't feel like sleeping in my own bed tonight. I pulled back her duvet and climbed in beside her, chucking her teddy bear out of the way to make more room. Her bed was nice and warm but it still took me ages to fall asleep. I just couldn't stop worrying about what was going to happen tomorrow.

I woke up really early the next morning – the clock said it was six o'clock – and when I went downstairs Mum was up and wide awake, trying on a dress she'd bought in London. The dress was a long shimmery one with pink sequins and it came with a pink feather boa. She'd bought loads of other clothes as well. They were all over the floor.

'I thought you went to find Kate,' I said. 'Not to go shopping.'

'She wasn't in,' Mum said. 'This shop was open late. They wanted to close up, but I just kept buying things!' She giggled.

'So, are you not going to bother about Kate now then?' I asked hopefully.

'I'm going back today.'

'To London?'

She nodded as she struggled to do up the zip on her dress. She had a red bra underneath that was nearly all showing because the front of the dress was so low cut. 'Look! It's the school colours!' she giggled, pulling a pair of red, lacy knickers out of a carrier bag and twirling them round her finger.

'Mum, you can't go back to London!' I barked at her. 'And you can't wear that. It's disgusting and it doesn't even do up!'

'I don't need it to do up,' Mum laughed. 'I need it to undo. In a striptease you undo!'

'*Striptease?*' I felt like I was going to be sick.

She picked up the feather boa and started whirling it round her head like she was about to throw it into an imaginary audience along with the knickers.

'Mum, that's not funny!' I protested.

She started talking nonsense – at least it seemed like nonsense to me. '. . . bring the house down . . . the school down . . . the world down . . .' She was dancing round the room in the dress, swinging her hips and twirling her feather boa and humming music that sounded like the kind you might dance to if you were a stripper, instead of being somebody's mother and headmistress of a school.

Mum was dancing her way into the kitchen, so I followed her. I stopped as I saw what she'd done in there. The cupboards were all open and cans and packets of food were lying around all over the work surfaces. Mum was heading for the back door. 'Mum

– no!' I rushed over and pulled the key out of the lock. 'Don't go outside now, *please*.'

'Please don't go,' Mum repeated after me. '*Pleeeease* don't go.' She sounded like she was thinking about breaking into song.

Martha suddenly appeared in the kitchen doorway. All the noise must have woken her up. I grabbed her by the arm and pulled her back out into the living room. I didn't want her to see Mum like this. 'Go back to bed!' I snapped. 'It's too early to get up yet!'

Martha glared at me. 'I want to see Mummy!'

'Listen, Martha, you've got to do what I say! I'm in charge until Dad gets back!'

'No, you're not!' She screwed up her nose. '*Mummy* is!'

That's when I really lost it. 'Oh, sure she is!' I bawled. 'She's *really* in charge of us, isn't she? If she wants to throw *you* into the sea, along with all your goldfish, is that OK?'

Martha's face crumpled and she burst into tears.

I felt really bad then – as if all my angry feelings had swirled up into a big ball which I'd just hurled full-on at Martha. And I hadn't got rid of them that way either. They had just bounced straight back to me, only now I'd hurt Martha with them as well. And all because I didn't know what to do.

I told Martha I was sorry and got her to come upstairs with me by whispering that we were going to make a special secret phone call to Dad. On the way upstairs I lifted the front-door key off the key rack, made sure the door was double-locked so there was no way Mum could open it, and put the key in my dressing-gown pocket. I let Martha ring Dad's number, but there was *still* nobody there even though a whole day had passed since I'd last phoned and it was early evening in New Zealand now. I tried not to let my sister see how worried I was.

I told her to get dressed and that I'd bring her breakfast upstairs to her, and then I went to get dressed myself.

When I got downstairs, Mum was sitting on the sofa still wearing her new pink outfit. She had found a pair of knitting needles and she was un-ravelling one of her jumpers into a long string of red wool.

'Mum, what are you doing?' I asked, staring at the half-unpicked jumper on her lap.

'Knitting,' she said. 'Knitting backwards . . . Mum used to knit. Babies aren't always good sleepers.'

I kept staring at her. I was remembering some-thing Dad had told me once when I'd asked what Mum had been like when she was mentally ill. As usual, he had refused to talk about Mum's illness in very much detail. But he had said something about mentally ill people often not making any sense when you were speaking to them.

Mum wasn't making any sense now. And all that stuff about Kate didn't make any sense either.

Suddenly I knew that I was going to have to phone Dr White whether I wanted to or not.

I waited until eight o'clock, then I went to use the phone in Mum and Dad's bedroom. Maybe Dr White would have started work by now. Dad used to be at work by eight when he was doing a surgery before we'd moved. I didn't tell Mum what I was doing. I would tell Dr White that Mum wasn't making sense, but I would also tell him that she wasn't *mad* like some of his patients, because she knew who she was and she wasn't hearing voices or anything, so surely she didn't need to go back into hospital? I had to wait ages while the hospital switchboard put me through to the right department and, when they eventually did, Dr White's secretary wasn't in yet. Dr White wasn't in yet either. The switchboard lady asked if I wanted them to page him. I said I did and I hung on for what seemed like forever until she came back to me. 'I'm sorry, dear. He's not responding. He might be on his way in to the hospital. Why don't you try again in half an hour or so? Or there's the duty doctor if it's an emergency . . . Is it an emergency?'

I told her I would wait and try Dr White again a bit later and put down the phone. I didn't want to speak about Mum to a doctor I didn't know.

'Mum!' I called downstairs. She didn't answer, so I went to find her. She wasn't in the living room and when I went through to the kitchen she wasn't there either, but the kitchen window was wide open. A chair was pulled up against it. I unlocked the door, rushed outside and checked our driveway. Mum's car was gone.

I felt sick. Had she gone to London again? Or, worse still, had she gone to school wearing that dress? It was Tuesday. Mum had a meeting with the deputy head first thing every Tuesday.

I was having trouble breathing properly and I

couldn't think what to do, and then I thought of something – Mum's mobile! I rushed back into the house and rang the number. I held my breath as it started ringing out. There was a voice at the other end, crackly but audible. 'Mum, is that you?' I gasped. 'Where are you?'

'It's Martha.'

'Martha!' I was so confused, I couldn't think for a few moments. Martha wasn't with Mum. Martha was here with me. Martha was upstairs in her room. 'Martha, where are you?'

'In the car . . . Mummy's taking me to London . . . I wanted you to come too, but she said—'

'Put her on!' I gasped. 'Quickly!'

There was a brief crackle as if the phone was being handed over, and then the line went dead.

I quickly punched in Mum's number again, but now her phone was just on voicemail. I was about to try a second time when our own phone rang out. I slammed the receiver against my ear. '*Mum?*'

'It's Dad.'

'Dad!' I couldn't believe it.

'Daniel, I've only just got back to the house,' he said. 'Grandma died a couple of hours ago. What's wrong?'

'It's Mum,' I blurted. 'She stopped taking her medicine. She's taking Martha to London. I'm scared what she'll do. She thinks Martha isn't really her baby. She thinks she was swapped in the hospital. Dad, it's not true, is it? Martha is our baby, isn't she? She couldn't really have been swapped—' I broke off because I was starting to cry.

There was a silence at the other end. Then Dad started asking questions rapidly, but I couldn't answer any of them. I felt like *my* brain was going completely mad too. All I knew was that if anything happened to Martha – or Mum – I couldn't stand it. I started saying that to Dad, over and over, not listening to him at all.

'DANIEL, SHUT UP!' Dad barked, and I got such a jolt that I did shut up.

I listened as he gave me a set of instructions. I was to give him Dr White's telephone number. Dad would phone him from New Zealand. While he was doing that, I was to ring '999' and call the police and tell them my mum was mentally ill and had driven off in the car with my little sister.

'But she's not really *ill*,' I protested. 'And I know where she is. She's gone to see that lady called Kate who we met who was in hospital with her . . . the one she thinks—' I gulped. I couldn't even bear to say out loud again what Mum thought. 'Kate lives in London. Mum went to see her yesterday but she wasn't in.'

'Daniel, how has Mum been acting towards Martha recently?' Dad sounded very tense now.

'OK. Not horrible or anything. Just staring at her sometimes—'

Dad interrupted again. 'Do you have this woman's address?'

'No. Mum got it from the bed-and-breakfast place.'

'What bed-and-breakfast place?'

'Where Kate was staying when she was here. It was on Castle Road.' I tried really hard to think of the name.

Dad said not to phone the police after all because he would do that. 'But I do want you to contact a grown-up to come and be in the house with you. Phone Sally's mother, OK?'

'But—'

'Daniel, just *do* it! I'll phone you again when I've got hold of Mum's doctor.' He put down the phone.

I didn't understand what was happening any more. Dad must think things were really serious to have decided to call the police. But even though Mum was upset and acting strangely, she would never do anything *dangerous*, would she?

The doorbell rang.

'Don't look pleased to see me or anything, will you?' Abby said as I opened the front door.

I was staring at her with an undisguised look of disappointment on my face. I'd thought for a second that she might be Mum, that's all. 'Sorry,' I said quickly. 'It's just . . . something's happened . . .'

'*What?*' Abby asked, frowning.

'It's . . . It's . . .' And I pulled her inside and blurted everything out.

Abby didn't look shocked or like doing a quick about-turn, which is how I reckon *I'd* feel if some kid I hardly knew suddenly poured out all that stuff to me the very first time I called in for him on my way to school. But then, I guess Abby was different from me. She'd already gone through a lot of scary stuff with her own mother. 'Listen, try not to worry,' she said quickly. 'The police are bound to find her. But . . .' She stopped there.

'But *what?*' I demanded.

'Well, I was thinking. Maybe if we found out the

116

address where she's gone then we could give it to the police and they could find her quicker. Are you sure you can't remember the name of that B. & B.?'

I shook my head. 'All I can remember is that it was on Castle Road.'

'Right.' She went over and picked up our phone.

'What are you doing?'

'Phoning for a taxi. You don't want to just sit here doing nothing, do you?'

'But my dad said to stay put.'

'*So?* Your dad's in New Zealand, isn't he?'

I frowned. She was right, of course. Dad wasn't in any position to stop me.

We got the taxi to take us to Castle Road, which was in the old part of town. It was raining and I had to hold my hood up against the wind as I started to walk along the road looking for B. & B. signs in people's windows. Abby crossed the road to check out the other side.

We'd got about halfway up the street when a police car pulled up on the road, level with us. The siren wasn't on, but the blue light was flashing. The policeman who was driving wound down his window. 'Are you Daniel MacKenzie?' he asked me.

My heart skipped a beat. Maybe they'd already found Mum and Martha. I nodded. 'Have you found my mum?'

'Not yet, but we're working on it. Come on. Get in the car. You're soaked.'

'I know where Mum is,' I said, not moving. 'She went to see this lady in London. There's a B. & B. here that has her address.'

'We're dealing with that. You shouldn't have run

off like that, mate. Your dad's really worried about you. When he couldn't get you on the phone again, he told us to look for you here.'

'I'm not going home,' I said. 'I have to keep looking.'

'If you get in the car, we'll have a look together. OK?'

'OK.' I called over to Abby and we both climbed into the back of the car. 'Drive slowly so we can see the numbers,' I said. As we drove up to the top of the road, I stared at the houses on my side. Most of the numbers were displayed: 52 . . . 54 . . . 56 . . . 58 . . . The house after Number 58 had a B. & B. sign in the window and it said *Mariner's Cottage* in blue paint above the front door. 'Stop!' I shouted, nearly leaping out of my seat. 'That's it! That's it! That's the one!' And I only realized how much I was shaking when Abby put her hand on my shoulder like she was reaching out to calm a spooked horse.

The police took over after that and, while they worked to locate Mum, I had to wait at the police station. They phoned Dad to tell him I was safe and one of the officers spoke to him for several minutes in private before coming through to fetch me so that I could speak to him too.

'Dad, we found out where Mum went,' I said as soon as I was given the phone. 'The police in London are going to find her. But they say she might have to go to hospital.'

'I know,' Dad said. 'They've just told me that.'

'But Mum hates hospitals, Dad. She'll freak out if she has to go back to one.'

'They'll look after her in hospital, Daniel. She'll be safe there. There's no need to be scared about that.' He sounded like he thought there was something *else* to be scared about, but before I could ask him he was saying, 'I've phoned the school and spoken to the deputy head. I've explained to him why your mother and you weren't in school today. And I've booked the earliest flight home that I can. Hopefully I should get back the day after next. Until I get there, do you think Sally's mother would look after you?'

'I'm not staying at Sally's!'

'Daniel, there's nowhere else.' Dad sounded stressed.

'There's Abby's,' I blurted out. Abby was still with me at the police station. The police had called Susie, who'd said it was OK for her to stay and keep me company for a bit. 'Her sister looks after her but her sister's a grown-up. Please can I stay with her, Dad? Then I won't have to tell everything to Sally's mum. She's really gossipy,' I added quickly. (I didn't have a clue if Sally's mum was gossipy or not, but I knew that saying that might just swing it with Dad, because he *really* hates strangers knowing about Mum's illness.)

'Well—'

'Abby says her sister won't mind. You can ask her yourself. Abby's got her work number, so you can phone her and speak to her. Please, Dad?'

'Well,' Dad still sounded unsure. 'The social worker will be there soon. Let's see what they think.' The police had already explained that they had phoned the duty social worker because they had to do that when children didn't have an adult there to look after them. The social worker would help sort out where Martha and I could stay until Dad got back. Assuming they *found* Martha before Dad got back . . .

'Dad, everything's going to be all right, isn't it?' I asked him, hearing my voice tremble slightly. Lots of ridiculous, scary thoughts had been going through my head since Mum and Martha had left the house this morning. Any second now Dad was going to confirm just how ridiculous they were.

Dad paused for longer than I'd expected him to. 'The police are doing everything they can, Daniel. They'll let us know as soon as they find them.'

Which didn't answer my question . . .

'Yes, but—'

'Daniel, I'll be there with you just as soon as I can,' Dad interrupted me. His voice sounded trembly too, all of a sudden. 'Put the police officer on again now, there's a good boy.'

I had a big lump in my throat as I handed the phone over. I knew the answer to my question now, even though Dad hadn't given it to me. The truth was that Dad didn't know if everything was going to be all right any more than I did.

12

The social worker who came to see me at the police station knew Susie and Abby already, and she seemed to think pretty highly of Susie. She told Dad that when she spoke to him on the phone.

Abby had already rung Susie, who'd agreed to look after me, so Dad phoned her and must have decided he trusted her, because pretty soon it was all arranged. Susie even got away early from work so she could come and collect us straight away from the police station. I was still really worried about Mum and Martha, but the police promised to come and tell us as soon as they knew anything and while we in the kitchen having tea, a police car pulled up outside. They told us that the police in London had found Mum and Martha at Kate's house. They were both safe and Mum had been taken to hospital. Martha was being brought back here.

I had this funny reaction when I heard. I couldn't seem to feel anything at all at first – nothing like I'd imagined I'd feel anyway. It was as if my brain wasn't connected to the rest of me or something, because I was hearing Mum and Martha were safe, and registering that they were, only my heart didn't feel any different at all. I smiled and all that, because people were watching me, but it wasn't until a good ten minutes later, when I was on my own in the bathroom, that it seemed to really sink in. The waiting was over. Mum and Martha hadn't died or had a car crash or any of the other things that had been going through my head all day until now. They were both safe and it wasn't just up to me to look after them any more. I stared at myself in the bathroom mirror and let the news sink in. I could see my face visibly relaxing in the mirror. I could see my fist punching the air as I mouthed, '*Yes!*' I wasn't going to shout it out loud though, because this moment wasn't for sharing with anyone else. This feeling was mine and only mine – the feeling of relief that Mum and Martha hadn't come to any harm today, even though I hadn't handled things very well when it *had* been my job to look after them.

Later, the social worker dropped Martha off. I wanted to give my sister a massive hug, but I didn't want to scare her by making her think I'd been worried about her, so I just gave her an ordinary one instead. I had lots of questions to ask her about what had happened at Kate's house. I held back until I'd taken her upstairs to show her where she was going to sleep and the two of us were on our own, but Martha didn't have much to tell me. She'd been sent upstairs to play with Sophie while Mum talked to Kate, and soon after that the police had come and been very kind to her while they explained that Mum wasn't well and needed to go and see a doctor in the hospital. Martha started asking *me* loads of questions then, about what was wrong with Mum, and when she would be coming home, and whether we were going to get to visit her in the hospital, and if so should we take her flowers or grapes or both. I couldn't answer most of her questions, but fortunately she got sidetracked by suddenly remembering something else.

'Mummy took some photos to show Kate and she gave them to me to look after,' she said. 'So I showed them to Sophie and she showed me her baby photos and we did a swap.' She handed me a photograph of Kate and Mum and the two babies, but where the babies didn't have knitted jackets and bonnets on. 'Kate and Mummy look really nice because the hairdresser had just been round to do everybody's hair.'

I looked at it. Mum did look nice. She looked happy and normal. Mum was holding Martha wrapped in a pink blanket, but this time the baby's head was uncovered.

I stared at it.

The baby Mum was holding – the baby that was supposed to be Martha – had dark hair. *Dark* hair. Not fair hair like Martha. Mum was right. Kate's baby was the one with fair hair. Unless . . . I turned the photo over to look at what was written on the back. It was just possible that Mum was holding Kate's baby in the picture and vice versa. But on the back, written quite clearly, Kate had put, *Me with Sophie, and Isobel with Martha, four days old.*

I turned the picture back over and stared from it to my sister.

'What's wrong?' Martha asked.

*

123

I hid the photograph that evening. I didn't want anyone else knowing about this. Not until I'd had a chance to ask Dad about it.

'The babies were swapped,' Mum had said, and nobody had believed her. Even I hadn't believed her. But what if she was right? I mean, the baby in the picture didn't look anything like Martha – it *couldn't* be her – even though it must have been the baby Mum had just given birth to.

I couldn't get to sleep that night for thinking about it. Abby was sharing Susie's bed tonight, while Martha slept in her bed and I had a camp bed on the floor next to her. I wished I could tell Abby what was on my mind, but I knew that I couldn't.

I tried to stop feeling so scared but it was difficult. I mean, I had a dad who was on his way home to me right now, and a mum who was great when she was well. So I don't know why I felt like my whole world was falling apart. Except that I also had a sister who might not be my sister.

I climbed out of my bed and into Martha's. There was no teddy to evict this time because he was still at home. Susie had promised we could go and fetch him tomorrow. I buried my face in Martha's silky blonde hair and took a deep breath. Maybe if I tried I could *breathe* her in so that nobody would ever be able to take her away from me.

The next morning I told Susie I didn't want to go to school. I couldn't imagine what they must be saying at school about Mum. I didn't see how either Mum or I could ever go back there again. I thought I'd end up having an argument with Susie about it, but I was wrong. She sent Abby to school and took Martha because she actually wanted to go, but then she said I could come to work with her today if I liked.

Susie worked in a little shop that sold antique furniture. 'Now, Daniel, just don't *touch* anything, OK?' Susie said when we got there.

I promised I wouldn't, but I knew it was going to be difficult.

At lunchtime I was absent-mindedly fiddling with one of the drawers in this posh antique desk when a lady came into the shop who reminded me of Mum. She had long dark hair and big eyes and she was plump in a nice curvy sort of way. I suddenly wanted to see Mum really badly, or at least to know how she was.

I asked Susie if we could phone the hospital. Mum had been brought back from London so that Dr White could look after her on one of his wards. I kept trying to forget how I'd promised her that she'd never have to go back inside that hospital again, no matter what.

'I don't know if they'll let us speak to her, but we can ring up the ward and see how she is,' Susie replied. She rang the hospital and asked what ward Mum was on. 'OK, so can you put me through to Elizabeth Ward, please?'

'*Elizabeth* Ward?' I felt my eyes start to prick. That was the ward where all those awful mad people had been. 'I don't want to speak to her after all,' I said, running out of the shop.

Susie joined me outside a few minutes later. She was holding my coat. 'Put this on or you'll catch cold.'

'Dad says you catch cold through germs, not through cold weather,' I grunted dismissively.

'Is that right? Well, maybe there are some germs about just waiting for a nice shivery person to inhabit,' Susie replied firmly. 'Put it on.'

I did as I was told. I'm used to doing as I'm told, I guess. Even now, when I really didn't feel like doing anything that anyone else asked me to do, here I was being my usual obedient self.

Susie told me that she'd spoken to the ward manager and found out that Mum was having a nice long sleep at the moment.

'She hasn't slept properly in ages,' I told her.

'That's good then, isn't it?'

'I can't see what's good about Mum being on a ward full of psychos!' I was angry with her for looking at me like she felt sorry for me. 'You must be used to that with *your* mum, aren't you?' I added.

Susie kept her voice steady. 'I've visited my mother on a psychiatric ward, yes.' She looked like she was thinking of saying something else on the topic, but she didn't. 'Come on. I'm allowed to close up the shop for half an hour. Let's go and get some lunch.'

'I don't want any lunch!'

She ignored that and started doing up the buttons on my coat for me as if I was two years old instead of twelve, and I just stood there like a two year old letting her. It was weird but it actually felt quite comforting to be treated like a little kid who wasn't in charge of anything, not even the doing up of their own buttons. It was much better than being expected to know what to do all the time as if you were a grown-up. I looked up at Susie's face then, suddenly not feeling angry with her any more, as I realized that she probably knew exactly how I felt.

I spent one more day at the shop and Martha spent one more day at school before Dad finally arrived home. I reckon both of us were counting the hours the whole time, working out how much longer it was going to be until we saw him. I kept telling myself that as soon as Dad got home he would explain everything about Martha and the baby photographs and it would all become clear again. And yet, what if Dad didn't know about this either?

As soon as the doorbell rang on Thursday evening, Martha and I raced to the door.

'Daddy!' Martha screamed as she charged into his arms.

'Daddy!' I blurted too before I could stop myself, but I didn't care if I sounded like a baby, I was just so glad to have him back.

Martha was cuddling Dad, looking happier than I'd seen her look in ages, as if now that Dad had walked back in through the door all our troubles had magically vanished into thin air.

Only they hadn't. But then she didn't know everything, did she?

We took Dad through to the living room. Susie and Abby went to make a pot of tea in the kitchen while Martha and I sat next to Dad on the sofa. Martha was asking questions non-stop, and I found myself noticing all the things about Dad again that I'd already spent years noticing, especially his hands. Like the way the veins on the backs of his hands stand out and make a V shape. And how he has a mole on his left wrist just below his watch strap. There were other things that were different though. His face was thinner and his hair looked like it had more grey bits in it than I remembered from before. He hadn't shaved and he had dark circles under his eyes. It was only later that I thought about how bad he must be feeling, with his mother dying and then this happening to Mum. Right then I was only thinking about how *I* felt.

We sat drinking tea and talking politely for twenty minutes or so. Then Dad thanked Susie for looking after us, and I was just getting ready to go upstairs to collect my stuff, when Dad asked if Susie would do him one more favour. He wanted to go straight up to the hospital to see Mum and he wondered if we could stay on at Susie's place while he did that. He would come back and collect us afterwards. I felt funny when he said that. I don't know why. I mean, of course he had to see Mum. I just didn't see why he had to do it right now, that was all, when we'd only just got him back again. Susie said that was fine and Dad said he'd call a taxi and go straight there.

'Dad, they've put Mum on this horrible ward up at the hospital,' I warned him.

'I'm sure Doctor White knows what he's doing, Daniel. It's your mum's safety that matters most at the moment, not her surroundings.'

I hadn't said it to criticize Dr White, but now I suddenly *did* feel critical. Dad might not care about Mum's surroundings, but *I* did. 'I don't see how safe she is on a ward with a whole load of mad people,' I spat out, 'but go and see it if you don't believe me.'

'Daniel . . . Mum's getting the best possible care—'

'How can you tell? You haven't seen her, have you? You've been in New Zealand!'

Dad looked taken aback. 'I know you want her back again, Daniel, but we have to be patient.' He got up to phone for his taxi.

'Daddy, I don't want you to go,' Martha said, trying to pull him back down on to the sofa again. Her face was crumpling up.

'Mummy needs me to go and see her, sweetheart,' he told her gently.

Martha started to cry. 'I don't want you to go!'

'I'll be back soon, Martha, I promise.'

Suddenly I felt really angry. 'Don't say *that* to her!' I shouted, jumping up from the sofa. 'Tell her *exactly* what time you're going to be back! *Exactly!*'

I stopped abruptly. Everyone was staring at me.

13

That night Dad came into my bedroom as I was getting ready for bed. 'How are you doing, kiddo?' Calling me *kiddo* had been a bit of a joke between us a year or so back. Mum hated it and said that both Dad and I were watching too many American movies.

'I'm OK. Dad . . .' I felt sort of achy inside all of a sudden as if, now that he was back, it was really hitting me how much I had missed him while he was away. 'Is Aunt Helen angry with us?'

'Why would she be angry?'

'Because you had to come back before the funeral.'

'Of course she's not angry. She understood that I had to come home. The important thing was being there with Grandma before she died. Actually, she's feeling really guilty for not listening to you when you tried to tell her Mum was getting poorly. She didn't tell me about your phone call at the time and now she wishes she had.'

I looked at him. He looked terrible. His face was all saggy and his eyes were red. He looked like he was the one who was sick, not Mum. But I still had to ask him this.

I swallowed. 'Dad . . .' I had to ask him even though I was almost too scared to hear the answer. 'Is there other stuff you and Mum haven't told me?' My voice went hoarse. 'Stuff about Martha?'

'What do you mean?'

'Dad, look at this.' But just as I was about to show him the photograph I hadn't dared show anyone else until now, the phone started ringing.

'Wait a minute, Daniel. It might be the hospital.' He hurried through to his bedroom to answer it.

'*Who?*' I heard Dad say. 'Oh, right. *Kate.*'

I immediately got out of bed and went out on to the landing so I could hear better. It was just as well I did, because Dad closed the bedroom door before he carried on speaking in a low voice. 'Well, she's in good hands now at least. No, the children are OK. Well, as OK as can be expected.' He listened for a bit longer. 'I don't think so, no . . . It's OK . . . No, she didn't, but don't worry . . . Yes, I'm happy to leave it as it is . . . If you still feel it's the right thing for us to keep yours, that is . . .'

I leaned back against the landing wall, scarcely able to breathe. *If you still feel it's the right thing for us to keep yours.* What did that mean? Did it mean that there *had* been a swap in the past that they both knew about?

I hurried back into my bedroom as I heard Dad put down the phone. Nothing in my life was making sense any more. I sat down on my bed and looked at the photograph. Had the swap Mum had talked about really happened after all? Was it true that Martha really was Kate's daughter and Sophie really belonged to *my* family?

Dad stuck his head round my door. 'That was Kate asking how Mum is.'

I knew I had to ask him about it, no matter how scared I was to hear the answer. I took a deep breath. 'I heard you on the phone, Dad,' I said. 'I heard you talking about the . . .' I swallowed. '. . . about the swap.'

Dad didn't react how I'd thought he would. 'Oh, you know about that, do you?' He didn't seem particularly surprised that I knew or even like the subject was such an important one. 'I wish you wouldn't sneak about listening to other people's private conversations, Daniel. Yes, we were talking about the swap. Kate was worrying about it and I told her not to. Martha's happy. Sophie's happy. I don't want to upset them if we don't have to.'

Suddenly Martha's voice came from the other room. 'Daddy!' She sounded scared, as if she'd just had a bad dream or something.

'I'm coming, sweetheart!' Dad called out to her. He looked at me with narrowed eyes. 'I don't want you mentioning this to Martha, OK? I don't want her getting all upset about it.'

'But, Dad—'

'I mean it, Daniel. Put out the light now and get some sleep.'

I got into bed and switched off the light, but I had never felt so bewildered and let down in my whole life. And I knew I wouldn't be able to get to sleep easily that night.

I found that I was too scared to ask Dad again about what he'd told me. He spent most of the next day

132

sleeping. He didn't put up a fight about me going back to school. It was Friday and next week was half-term. I reckon he didn't think another day off would do much harm and it didn't seem to enter his head that I wouldn't want to go back *after* half-term either.

I kept thinking about what he'd said. Sometimes I reckoned I couldn't have heard him right, but then I reran our conversation in my head and I knew that I had. My main worry was that Martha might get taken away from us. And then there was the fact that Martha obviously knew nothing about any of this. I mean, she was going to find out one day and then how would she feel? I thought about what Mum had told me – that the swap must have happened when that mad lady took the babies off the ward. If both Mum and Kate were mentally ill then maybe that's why they didn't notice at the time, but the whole thing still seemed really weird to me.

When had Dad and Kate found out the truth? And why had they decided that they didn't want to swap the babies back again? And what about Mum? What about what *she* had wanted?

I had a lot more questions, but no time seemed to be the right time to ask them – even after Dad had recovered from his jet lag and had stopped falling asleep whenever he sat down.

Over the next few days I tried a few times to bring up the subject when Martha wasn't around, but as soon as I started, Dad and I seemed not to be able to connect up. It was almost as if we were talking about two separate things.

'Dad, you know what Kate and you were talking

133

about on the phone . . . the swap . . . ?' I began one day when Martha was round at Sally's house.

Dad looked at me as if he suspected I was trying to stir up trouble. 'I've told you, Daniel. I don't want you getting Martha all upset.'

'But, Dad—'

'Just drop it, OK?' he snapped, and he turned his back on me and left the room.

I stared after him, biting my lip. Dad was starting to seem more and more of a stranger to me since he'd come home, and less and less like the father I'd known before he left for New Zealand.

It was half-term and Susie had the week off work, so I spent quite a bit of time at her place while Dad went to visit Mum. Abby took me down to the park to play football with her and her friends and I met Rachel's brother, Michael. We hit it off really well and he invited me back to his place to watch his video of the World Cup. Michael said that Abby and Rachel were pretty good football players considering they were girls, and that got Abby all fired up saying that girls were just as good at football as boys and getting Rachel to agree with her. Thankfully she didn't try to get me to agree with her, because then she might have ended up falling out with me as well as with Michael. I didn't tell any of them how worried I was about Martha.

Martha either came with me or went round to Sally's. Nobody suggested that we visited Mum yet and I just assumed it was going to be the same now as it had been when I was little. Mum would be too ill for us to visit her for most of the time she was in hospital and we wouldn't see her again until she was nearly ready to come home. I tried not to think how long it might be before that happened.

Towards the end of the week Dad started to talk about me going back to school. He had spent quite a bit of time talking to the deputy head over the last week, and the school had been making arrangements to cover Mum's post. They were going to keep the job open for her for the moment and in the mean time our deputy head would be acting head. An announcement to the effect that Mum was unwell was going to be made in assembly, and the teachers had been instructed to be extra-supportive of me when I first went back. Dad seemed to think that I was going to be satisfied with that.

Well, he was wrong. I told him there was no way I was going back to that school after everything that had happened with Mum there. Besides, I reckoned I'd sort of grown *out* of school over the last few weeks and I told him that. I mean, I didn't see why I should have to do all the stupid work the teachers set when I knew now that there was more important stuff going on in the outside world. Dad said I was being silly. He said that everyone had to go to school in order to prepare themselves for the outside world, and how did I think all the doctors and nurses who were looking after Mum had got to be doctors and nurses if it wasn't through going to school?

'Anyway,' he added firmly. 'You're only twelve. You have to go back. It's the law.'

'Well, I want to change schools then.' I was lifting one of Mum's ornaments off the mantelpiece and fiddling with it as I spoke.

'Daniel—'

'You should have let me go to a different school in the first place. I told you it would all work out badly.' I put down the ornament with a bit of a bang. I really didn't see what right he had to be telling me what to do. Not now that I knew what *he* had done.

'Daniel, none of us could have predicted that this would happen.'

'I don't see why not. She's been ill before, hasn't she?' I picked up a glass candlestick and started to roll it about in my hand.

'Daniel, put that down.' He waited for me to put the candlestick down before adding carefully, 'It's been years since your mother had a manic episode.'

'A manic episode?' It was the first time I'd heard him use that word.

Dad nodded. 'That's what's been wrong with Mum. It was what was wrong with her when she was pregnant with Martha too. That's why she had to go into hospital then. Mania is like the opposite of depression. You get high in your mood instead of low, only it doesn't always feel good, because you can't sleep and everything speeds up inside your head. Sometimes you start losing touch with reality, so you think you're more important than you really are, which was what you saw happening with Mum.'

'So the way Mum acted at school was because of that?'

'That's right. She thought she was more and more important the sicker she got. In the end it sounds as though she thought she was the queen of the school instead of just the headmistress. She's got an illness called manic depression, which means that her mood isn't as stable as other people's. Bipolar mood disorder is its other name. *Bipolar*, see?'

I stared at him blankly. I didn't see. I'd waited years for him to give me any information at all about Mum's illness and now I felt like he was giving me too *much* information to take in.

'Bipolar because there are two opposite *poles* – depression and mania,' Dad explained. 'Think of it as like the North Pole and the South Pole – you're either feeling on top of the world or at the bottom of it.'

I frowned at him. I still didn't understand as well as I wanted to. 'I thought you could tell really easily if someone was mentally ill,' I said. 'But with Mum, I didn't know. I mean, she was acting weird but I didn't think she was . . . you know.' I couldn't bring myself to actually say the word *mad*.

'Everybody gets mentally ill in different ways, Daniel. And it's not always easy to pinpoint exactly when it starts happening.'

'Dad, why are you telling me all this now?' I asked him. 'I thought you said it wasn't any of my business until I was a grown-up?'

'I didn't say *that*, Daniel. Come on.'

'Well, you should have told me more about Mum's illness when I was little,' I said stubbornly. 'Then I would have understood it better.'

Dad looked thoughtful. 'I've always believed that children should be protected from certain things for as long as possible.'

I didn't reply. I didn't think children *could* always be protected. Not from all the things Dad wanted to protect Martha and me from, at any rate. Like the fact that Martha and I weren't really even brother and sister.

*

137

I was watching *Neighbours* the next afternoon when they showed that mad coffee-shop bomber again. This time his family were talking to the doctor – the one who's a GP like Dad, but who always seems to be running the hospital as well whenever any of the other characters get admitted there. He was explaining that the treatment the doctors were giving the man wasn't working. He said there was one more medication left to try but it would mean the man having loads of blood tests to check his blood cells weren't being knocked off. Apparently that was one of the possible side effects of this medication – that it could kill off your blood cells.

'And what if that doesn't help?' the man's sister asked. (She was one of the regular characters and had only just discovered that the coffee-shop bomber was her long-lost brother.) They did a close-up shot of her looking all trembly.

'Then we may have to accept that he won't ever fully recover. If that happens he's going to need to live somewhere where he can be properly cared for,' the doctor replied.

I switched the TV off. I knew it was *Neighbours* and not real, but it was freaking me out all the same. What if Mum had to have some extra-strong medication that killed off her blood cells? Or what if she never fully recovered and had to go away somewhere to be looked after? What if I never saw my normal mum ever again?

I felt my throat closing up and my eyes starting to prick, and for the first time since Mum had gone into hospital I started to cry. I was on my own, so there was nobody to see me and I ended up bawling my eyes out like a baby.

Dad wouldn't drop the subject of school, and on Sunday night he said I had to start back the next morning with everybody else now that half-term had ended. If Martha was able to go to school, Dad said, then I should be able to go too.

'It's not the same for Martha,' I protested. '*She's* not going to the same school as Mum, is she? *She* won't have everyone coming up to her asking what it's like having a mum in the loony bin.'

'Well . . .' Dad said. 'It's true, they might say that . . . So what we need to do is plan what *you* could say back to them.'

'I told you! I'm not going to *be* there!'

'Daniel, you've got to go back to school some time and the longer you leave it the more difficult it's going to get.'

'I'm not going,' I said again.

'Look . . . after a week or two the fuss will blow over . . . The teachers will help you out and if any of the other children say anything, perhaps you could say Mum hasn't been well but she's recovering now. Or that she's had an illness which made her behave strangely but that she'll soon be back to normal. Or you might even tell them that you'd rather not talk about it . . . What sounds best to you?'

I screwed up my face and swore under my breath. Didn't he get it? I wasn't going back and he couldn't make me. He couldn't make me do anything I didn't want to do ever again.

'Don't swear at me, Daniel.'

'I wasn't swearing at you. I was just swearing.'

He sounded like his patience was wearing thin. 'You're going back to school tomorrow whether you want to or not. It's not up for discussion any more.'

'Fine,' I said like I didn't really care. I knew what I was going to do tomorrow anyway, and it didn't involve school.

Dad was waiting for me when I got home on Monday afternoon. 'Daniel, sit down,' he said sternly. 'I want to speak to you.'

I didn't sit down. I started walking round the room, tidying up. Martha had dumped her PE kit on the floor as soon as she'd got in and her nightie was still lying on the sofa where she'd left it that morning. 'This place is a tip,' I complained to Dad. Goodness knows what *he'd* been doing all day.

'It can stay a tip for a few minutes longer. Now, *sit*.' He sounded stern, and normally I would have done what he said at that point, but I was finding that I didn't feel like reacting very fast to Dad's instructions since I'd overheard him on the phone that night to Kate. 'Daniel!' He grabbed me by the arm and pushed me down on to the sofa. 'Will you please do as you're told?'

'I'm not a kid, Dad!' I glowered up at him.

'Excuse me, but last time I looked you were still twelve.'

'*So?*'

'So that's not exactly a senior citizen!' He was frowning. 'Daniel, I'm sorry I wasn't here when you needed me and I'm very proud of you for coping with things as well as you did. But I'm back now and you haven't grown up overnight, even if that's how it feels to you at the moment.'

I made a big effort to look like I wasn't listening – even though I was.

'I know you weren't in school today,' he went on. 'Mrs Lyle phoned and told me. So where did you go?'

I shrugged. 'Just around.' Abby had lent me the key to her house and I'd spent the day there watching videos, but I wasn't about to say that and get Abby into trouble.

'Not a good enough answer, I'm afraid, Daniel!'

I looked at him. It was scary how numb I felt inside. 'I told you I wasn't going back to that school.'

Dad stared at me for a moment or two. He looked anything but numb. His face was going red. 'I'm disappointed in you, Daniel. I thought you'd at least want to give it a try, for Mum's sake.'

'Mum doesn't have to go back there either.'

'What? And lose the position she's worked for years to achieve? She won't want that, Daniel. She'll want to go back to that school and show them what a good job she can do when she's well again – and I think you should be there to see it. And to support her,' he added.

'I thought she was meant to be the one supporting *me*?' I said. 'I thought parents were meant to support their children, not the other way round!'

Instead of coming back with an answer, he stayed silent. Now, *that* was scary.

The next day Dad surprised me by saying he'd given it some thought and decided that maybe where I went to school *was* something I should be allowed to choose for myself after all. He said if I really wanted to change schools, then he'd arrange that for me, but that he wanted me to think about it for a bit longer first.

Over the next few days I tried to think what was the best thing to do, but I couldn't really be bothered thinking about it, because I was thinking all the time about Mum. Dad had said Mum was too ill to have visitors at the moment but that he would take her letters and cards from us if we wanted to write some. Martha drew her lots of pictures and sent her a big get-well card, but I didn't feel like doing that. I mean, sending a get-well card was the sort of thing you did when someone was an ill version of themselves. With Mum, it was as if all that excess energy I'd watched building up inside her had finally blown the fuse that *kept* her being herself. So who would I be sending the card to? The person I *wanted* to send a card to – the person I thought about every night before I went to sleep and every morning as soon as I woke up – wasn't Mum as she was now. It was my *normal* Mum.

Then, on the Sunday evening, Dad surprised me by saying that he'd been thinking about it and maybe it was better if he took Martha and me to visit Mum after all, even though she wasn't completely back to normal yet.

'I thought you didn't think psychiatric hospitals were suitable places for children to visit,' I said, because that was what he'd always said in the past. I had always assumed that was the reason Dad hadn't taken me to see Mum all those years ago when I was only five and had been missing her really badly.

'Well, perhaps I was wrong,' Dad said. 'Perhaps if children are kept away they end up imagining something even worse than what's really there.'

I couldn't believe it. It seemed like Dad was the one whose brain had just received treatment, not Mum.

Martha was excited as Dad drove us up to the hospital that evening after tea. I had hardly been able to eat anything and now I was starting to feel even more nervous. It was nearly three weeks now since we'd seen Mum, and the nearer we got to the place the more uneasy I became. I was tugging at my seat belt to loosen it and unwinding my window and winding it up again and banging my feet against the plastic ledge where Dad keeps the maps and things until Dad got so fed up with telling me to sit still that he gave up. As we turned in through the gates, I suddenly blurted, 'Dad, I don't want to go inside.'

Dad glanced over at me. 'I'll be with you the whole time, Daniel. Nothing bad's going to happen. She got moved to a side room today, off the main ward, so we'll be able to see her without seeing any of the other patients.'

'I just don't want to go in there again, OK?'

Dad parked the car and undid his seat belt. 'Come on, Daniel. You'll regret it if you don't come in. Mum's expecting you.'

'I don't care,' I said. 'I just don't feel like seeing her right now.'

Dad looked taken aback. 'OK,' he finally said briskly. 'If that's how you feel. Keep the car doors locked and wait here until we get back.' I knew he was disappointed in me for saying that I didn't care and I felt a pang of guilt because I did care. I cared a lot.

I watched them walk into the building, Martha holding Dad's hand as she skipped along beside him. I looked up at the hospital windows in case Mum was looking out of any of them. She wasn't. I closed my eyes and tried to imagine her the way she looks when she's well, her long dark wavy hair tied back and her blue eyes alert and a bit intense-looking. Her voice was easy to hear inside my head. She always spoke very clearly and with a lot of feeling if she was talking about anything she cared about. I wanted to see Mum again really badly. But I knew now that I only wanted to see her when she was *that* person again. And if that never happened . . . I shuddered. I couldn't even bear to think about it.

14

A few days later I was watching *Neighbours* again when our doorbell rang. The mad bomber guy was struggling with the doctor who was trying to take his blood. The mad patient seemed just as crazy as he had done in the beginning, so it didn't seem like the especially strong medication had helped him at all. I wasn't meant to be watching *Neighbours*. I was meant to be doing some school work. I still hadn't made a decision about school and Dad was making me do school work at home now. He said I had until the end of the week to decide if I wanted to change schools or stay at my current one, but then he'd said that last week too. I'd never known Dad seem so uncertain about anything as he seemed now about my school situation. I hadn't told Dad my other major worry – that Mum would *never* go back to being her old self – because every time I thought about telling him, another thought stopped me. I thought how I couldn't trust him any more.

When I opened the door, Mrs Lyle was standing there holding a big pink envelope in her hand. Mrs Lyle was the last person I'd expected to see. I'd always thought she didn't like either Mum or me.

'Hello, Daniel,' she said. 'I've brought this round

for your mum. It's a get well card from all the teachers.'

'She isn't here,' I said. 'She's still in hospital.'

'I know, but we thought you could take it to her. We want her to know that we're all thinking about her. We didn't realize at the time, you see. That she was . . . well . . .' She flushed. 'None of the other teachers knew about her . . . her medical condition. If we'd known we'd have done more to help.'

'Daniel, who is it?' Dad came into the hall.

'One of my teachers,' I said, staring at Mrs Lyle, who I still couldn't imagine wanting to help my mother. Not unless it involved helping her into a straitjacket or injecting her with a syringe full of a tranquillizer or something.

'Well, invite her in, for goodness sake,' Dad said. He held out his hand to shake Mrs Lyle's. She said her first name when she introduced herself to him.

Dad showed her through to the living room and asked me to put the kettle on. I didn't. Instead I went outside to find Martha, who was bouncing a tennis ball against the side of the house. I felt like doing the opposite of what Dad told me to do most of the time now. We'd had lots of disagreements about stupid things like me leaving the milk out of the fridge when Dad kept telling me to put it away and me not going to bed on time and stuff like that.

'What was Mum like when you saw her the other night?' I asked Martha, grabbing the ball off her and starting to bounce it myself. I always feel better when I'm doing something with my hands.

This was the first time I'd asked her anything about the hospital visit and she eyed me warily, almost as if she knew she might get her head bitten off if she said the wrong thing. 'She was sleepy. I sang her a song and she said it was lovely.'

'Did she say anything weird?'

Before Martha could answer, the front door opened and Dad yelled out my name. I thought about running off and pretending I had already gone round to Abby's or something, but I wasn't allowed to leave the house without asking and I wasn't sure what Dad would do to me if I did. I'd heard him on the phone to Uncle Robert the other night saying how I was really testing the boundaries since he'd got back and how he was trying to stay cool but wasn't sure how much longer he was going to be able to stop himself from clobbering me. They had talked about Grandma too and Dad's voice had sounded choked, almost as if he were crying. Except that Dad never cries.

'I'm here!' I yelled, going back round to the front door, where Dad was waiting.

He didn't say anything about the kettle. 'Mrs Lyle's got something to tell you. Come inside for a minute.'

I couldn't think what Mrs Lyle could possibly have to tell me that I'd want to hear, but I followed him inside anyway. Mrs Lyle was sitting on the sofa. She looked up as I came in. 'Daniel, I wanted to tell you that we all really hope that you decide to come back to school soon. Everyone understands what you've been through and we all just want to help. Don't you think it's time to put a brave face on it and come back?'

I screwed up my nose. I'd need more than a

brave face to survive going back to school again. I'd need a suit of armour to hide inside and even that wouldn't be enough. Besides, I didn't trust her. I felt like I couldn't trust anybody any more. 'I don't need any help,' I said. 'So you can stop interfering!' And I ran out of the room.

'Daniel!' Dad called out after me, but I didn't turn back.

Up in my room I flung myself down on my tummy on my bed and wished I could turn back the clock to before we'd ever moved here. I wished I had never met Mrs Lyle or ever set foot in her stupid school. I was never going back there and I didn't want Mum going back there either.

There was a knock on my bedroom door.

'Go away!'

The door creaked open and I knew straight away that it was Dad. I wondered if this was the moment when he was going to do the clobbering.

I didn't get hit. Not even the slightest smack. Like I said before, smacking isn't Dad's style. I got a lecture, though. Dad said he didn't want me being rude to people who were already feeling guilty about the way they'd treated Mum. Now that Mrs Lyle knew that Mum had a mental illness she was being very understanding about the various changes Mum had tried to make up at the school, Dad said. And she had told him she would support Mum as much as she could when she came back. Dad said that a lot of people wouldn't be *more* understanding when they found out Mum was mentally ill – they'd be *less* so. So we should be grateful that Mrs Lyle – and at least *some* of the other members of staff – were reacting so positively now that they had been told about it.

'What about the ones who *aren't* reacting positively?' I asked.

'Mum can handle those people as long as she's got some support,' Dad said. He added that, although it would be hard, he thought Mum would want the opportunity to get back into school and face everyone again just as soon as she was able to.

'She might not,' I protested. 'She might be too embarrassed to *ever* go back!' And she might not ever be well enough to go back either, I thought.

Dad said not to get Mum's embarrassment mixed up with my own. Mum would need to get over what she'd done when she was ill, he said. And I would have to get over it too – and forgive her.

'She's got an illness, hasn't she?' I blurted out. '*She* can't help it! There's nothing to forgive *her* for!'

'Listen, Daniel,' he began slowly. 'I know you blame me for going off to be with Grandma and leaving you . . .'

'I don't blame you for that,' I said tersely, before he could continue.

'I think you do,' Dad replied. 'And I can understand why. But—'

'*That's* not what I blame you for!' I butted in, so frustrated I wanted to scream at him. Didn't he understand *anything*?

'What then?' he asked, looking as if he really didn't know.

'You shouldn't have let it happen. And you shouldn't have lied about it!' I was starting to cry now.

'Lied about what?'

'About Martha being Mum's baby when she isn't. Mum wasn't mad about that – she was *right*! And you knew that all along!'

Dad looked confused. 'Daniel, what are you talking about?'

'You knew the babies were swapped!' I yelled. 'You knew Martha and Sophie were swapped and you decided not to tell anyone. It's . . . It's . . .' But I couldn't put into words how betrayed I felt by the one person I had always completely trusted.

'Daniel, Martha wasn't swapped! Your mother was ill when she said that. It's just not true. I can't believe you think—'

'I heard you on the phone to Kate!' I shouted. 'You said as long as Martha and Sophie were happy it was OK. But it's not OK!'

Dad looked like he was trying to figure out what on earth I was getting at. Then, suddenly, light seemed to dawn. 'Are you talking about the photographs? Martha swapped a photograph with Sophie. She offered it to Sophie in exchange for one of ours. Kate was phoning to apologize and see if we wanted to swap them back, but I didn't see the point in making a big fuss and upsetting Martha.'

I stared at Dad. For once I was speechless. My head felt like it was spinning with overheard conversations, and horrible thoughts I had had about Dad, and everything Mum had said when she was ill. Everything was swirling around in my head and none of it seemed real any more.

'Listen, Daniel,' Dad said, frowning. 'I'd better get back to Mrs Lyle, but I think we ought to have a little talk about all this when she's gone, don't you?'

I'd got out the photograph which I had put at the bottom of one of my drawers because I hadn't wanted to look at it any more. Now I was sitting looking at it with Dad. 'In the photo Mum's baby has dark hair,' I pointed out shakily. 'That's why I thought it couldn't be Martha.'

'Martha was born with dark hair,' Dad explained. 'It fell out after the first month or two and when it grew back in again it was fair. It happens quite a lot – that a baby's hair falls out and grows back a different colour. Don't you remember that happening?'

I shook my head. I couldn't remember an awful lot about when Martha was a baby. Most of my memories started after Mum came back to live with us again.

'Martha is your sister, Daniel. There's no doubt about that. You weren't really questioning that, were you?'

Slowly it was starting to sink into place. Martha had had dark hair at the beginning and *then* she had become blonde. It was as simple as that. There was nothing to worry about. She *was* our baby after all. I felt light-headed with relief, as if I'd just been told I was free to go instead of getting sent to the electric chair or something.

And the best thing was that Dad hadn't lied to me. He was still the same dad I'd had when he'd left for New Zealand.

'But didn't Mum *know* that's what happened?' I

asked him. 'That Martha's dark hair fell out, I mean?'

'She didn't *see* it happening because she wasn't with Martha over that time, but I told her about it. She never questioned it until now. But I think she always had a sense that she'd lost the little dark-haired baby she remembered from the hospital. Maybe that feeling got stronger as she became ill. And seeing Kate must have triggered the thought that Kate had somehow taken her original baby away. People can start believing something is true that *isn't* true when they're mentally ill,' Dad added. 'Like believing they're the queen when they're not, or thinking someone has swapped their baby for a different baby when they haven't.'

'They sound like crazy thoughts to me,' I said.

Dad nodded slowly. 'That's one way of looking at it. But you know, I think those thoughts your mum had – even though they seemed crazy – came out of some *real* feelings she had about Martha.'

I frowned. 'I don't understand.'

'Your mother completely missed out on those first months of Martha's life. Martha had changed so much by the time she saw her again that she didn't even recognize her. Think what it must have been like for her. It must truly have been like being handed a completely different baby.' He shook his head sadly. 'She should have kept Martha with her in hospital.'

'Mum said *you* wouldn't let her keep Martha after what happened with that lady,' I said. 'After she took all the babies away.'

Dad looked at me. 'Mum told you about that?'

I nodded.

He sighed. 'It's true that all I wanted was to take Martha home after that happened, even though the staff sorted it out so quickly that the babies weren't really ever in danger. Your mother's psychiatrist wanted me to let her keep Martha with her. They even moved that other patient to another ward. But I felt too anxious about it to let Martha stay. I thought it would just be a week or two until your mother was well enough to come home again herself, anyway, but she suddenly got very depressed.' He looked at me. 'It took the doctors a long time to make her better from that. That's why she was in hospital for so long and I couldn't take you to see her.'

I stared at him. I had never heard this part of the story before. Now I knew why I hadn't got to see Mum when I was little for all that time.

15

The following morning, Dad started going on at me again to make a decision about school. I was just on my way upstairs to escape from him when the post arrived through our letter box. I bent down to pick it up. There was a letter for me. I didn't recognize the writing on the outside of the envelope at first. It was Dad who said, 'That looks like Mum's writing.'

I tore off the envelope and opened the card inside. My eyes went straight to the signature scrawled at the bottom, 'With love from Mum'.

'Let me see!' Martha said, but I shook her off.

'No, it's mine!' And I ran upstairs with it and shut myself in my room.

It was a card with an illustration from *Alice in Wonderland* on the front, a picture of the Mad Hatter's Tea Party. Mum had written inside in her slanty handwriting: *Dear Daniel, I found this in the hospital shop and I hope it makes you laugh. I can't wait to see you again so please come to see this Mad Hatter soon. With love from Mum.* There was a whole row of kisses.

I could almost see Mum in the hospital shop, laughing when she found that card. But the mother I was imagining doing that was Mum when she was well.

'Dad,' I shouted, running downstairs to show him. 'Look!'

Dad looked at the card and smiled too.

Martha had a look as well, but she didn't understand what it meant. She didn't understand that it was a special message from Mum – my old mum – to tell me that she was back again.

'I want to go and see her, Dad,' I said eagerly.

Dad nodded. He looked relieved. 'I'll take you up there today.'

In the car, on the way to the hospital, Dad took advantage of the fact that I was a captive audience. 'You have to make up your mind about school by the end of today,' he said firmly. 'Otherwise I'll decide for you, OK?'

I nodded. 'OK.' But secretly I felt sick inside. I just wanted to stay at home from now on and not have to face going back to school – *any* school – ever again. I was dreading having to make the choice Dad was forcing me to make, because neither secondary school sounded like a good option to me any more. But I couldn't say that to Dad.

Then he said something that surprised me. 'I told Grandma what a good report we got from your last school. She said to tell you to keep it up. I told her about that story you wrote last year that your teacher got you to read out in assembly. It really made her proud. Grandma used to write stories when she was young. Did you know that, Daniel?'

I shook my head. No one had mentioned that before. And then I had a sudden memory of Grandma telling me a story. It was the one time she'd come to England to stay with us. I had been about six at the time. I remember introducing her to Martha, saying, 'This is our baby. She cries a lot.' And a few days later Grandma had told me a story called, *The baby who wouldn't stop crying*. The baby in the story had a big brother who was very smart.

I suddenly wished Grandma wasn't dead, so I could send her one of my stories. Or that I'd sent her one when she was alive.

'I wish Grandma hadn't lived in New Zealand,' I said. 'I felt like I didn't have a grandma at all because she was so far away, but I did, didn't I?'

'Yes,' Dad said. From his hoarse voice and the way his eyes were suddenly welling up, I wondered if I'd said the wrong thing again. 'I should have taken you and Martha out there to see her more often. I'm sorry.'

I didn't know what to say to stop him looking so sad, apart from telling him that us not seeing Grandma very much wasn't his fault. After all, she was the one who had decided to emigrate to live near my aunt rather than us. But then, he was a grown-up, so he shouldn't need me to tell him things like that, should he?

'Daniel!' Mum was excited when she saw me, beaming as she held out her arms to give me a hug. Her eyes were all teary, which she said was a side effect of the medication she was on, but I thought she was just really emotional because she was seeing me again. I know *I* was.

Since Martha was at school, Dad said he would

leave us together for a bit while he went and did some shopping.

It was strange seeing Mum again now that some bits of her had gone back to normal and some bits hadn't. For instance, she was wearing her normal clothes again, not the really bright ones she'd worn before, and her hair was tied back just how she likes to wear it for work. And she was wearing make-up, but not too much. (She'd switched to wearing this really bright-red lipstick before.) She was talking normally for most of the time and everything she said made sense. But she was still a bit irritable, snapping at the nurse who came to give her her tablets, and yelling at a patient who barged into her room without knocking. She had been there for nearly a month now and Dr White had been giving her some new medication as well as putting her back on lithium.

'You must have been scared of me, Daniel,' she said, almost as soon as Dad left. 'All that rubbish I talked about Martha. I'm so sorry.'

'It's OK,' I said. 'You couldn't help it. But I'm really glad you're better now.' I gave her a shy smile. 'Thanks for sending me that card.'

She smiled back. 'I knew you'd like it. I know, let's go to the hospital shop now. They sell other things as well as cards. There's something funny I want to show you.'

So we went out into the main hospital together and she didn't seem scared like she had done when we'd come here before. And somehow, because she wasn't scared, neither was I. The thing she wanted to show me was the rows of ladies' knickers hanging up in the shop. I felt embarrassed when I saw them, especially as Mum was pointing and giggling at them. They were huge white and pink knickers like your granny would wear and Mum started telling the lady behind the counter how she felt really sorry for the patients in here who didn't have families to come and visit them and bring them their own knickers from home. I felt myself going bright red the longer she stayed on the subject of knickers, but Mum didn't seem to notice me squirming.

Mum wasn't completely back to normal. I could see that. She still giggled a bit too easily and she couldn't be bothered adding up our change in the shop, which is something she usually always does to check that it's right. And she let me buy Smarties even though she normally doesn't like me eating them because she reckons they make me hyperactive, even though they don't. No, she might not be completely back to her normal, bossy self yet, but she was getting there.

Dad was coming back after he'd been to the supermarket and as Mum and I sat in her room waiting for him, we fell silent. We were both perched on the edge of the bed facing the window. I was fiddling with the stuff on Mum's locker, but she didn't say anything, not even when I knocked her hairbrush on to the floor.

'Daniel, I'm sorry I stopped taking my lithium,' Mum said suddenly. 'It was stupid of me. I put all of us at risk. I don't know why I did it. I just started feeling that I was so well I didn't need it any more. Doctor White thinks that was the start of me going a bit high. He thinks I was actually a little bit ill *before* I stopped it. It was probably the stress of moving and the new job and Dad going away and everything that triggered that. The thing is, I *do* need it. It's kept me well for years. I can see that now.'

'It's OK—'

'It's not OK! It's not OK, at all!' She looked me straight in the eyes and added fiercely, 'Is it?'

I looked at her. OK, then . . . If she really wanted the truth . . .

'No!' I answered. 'It's *not* OK. It's been horrible!' I got off the bed and went to glare out at the cloudless blue sky.

Mum came over to the window too. She didn't speak, but she took hold of my hand and I didn't take it away.

After we'd stood like that for quite a long time, Mum asked tentatively, 'How's school? Has it been really awful for you?'

'I haven't been back to school,' I said. 'I might be going to the other secondary school here instead.'

'WHAT?' She made me jump, the way she shouted it.

'Dad says it's up to me to decide,' I said, backing away from her towards the door. 'Dad says I can change schools if I want. Hasn't he told you?'

'No, he hasn't told me! And there's no way you're changing schools! They have an appalling GCSE record at that other place and half the staff there are supply teachers!' As she said it, Dad came in the door behind me.

'What's wrong?' he asked, seeing Mum's face.

'Daniel's not changing schools!' Mum shouted at him.

'Izzy, he hasn't decided that for definite yet.'

'Malcolm, where he goes to school isn't his decision!' Mum snapped. 'It's ours!'

'Yes, but Daniel feels he's old enough now to help make that decision,' Dad said slowly. 'Especially after what's happened.'

'RUBBISH!' Mum snarled, and I knew that she definitely wasn't back to normal. If she was, she wouldn't be looking so agitated and she wouldn't be spitting as she spoke. Normally she had more control than that, no matter how angry she got.

'Izzy, let's discuss this later,' Dad said, quickly. 'It's time I took Daniel home. I'll ring you tonight.'

I stayed silent as we walked out of the building. As we headed across the car park, I said to Dad, 'Mum still isn't her normal self yet, is she?'

'Not completely, no.' He paused. 'But maybe she's right just the same. I mean, this decision about school *is* a parental one really. Mum and I looked at all the local schools before we moved here. We were convinced you'd miss out education-wise if we let you go to the other secondary school and I guess your mother feels that just as strongly now.'

'Yes, but it's still up to me to decide, isn't it?' I said stubbornly.

'Well, I'm beginning to think differently about that too, Daniel. I'm beginning to think it's not fair on you, asking *you* to make the choice. Maybe I gave in too easily when you first skipped school that day. Maybe I should just have taken you back there myself and given you no option but to get on with it. Maybe some decisions do still need to be taken by your parents when you're only twelve.' He looked at me solemnly. 'What do you think?'

'*You* tell *me*!' I snapped. 'Since you seem to reckon I *can't* think.' I stomped ahead to the car.

'Daniel, I'm not saying you can't think for yourself,' Dad said as he caught up with me. 'I'm just saying that maybe it's what Mum and I think that should count in this particular instance.'

'If what *Mum* thought always counted she'd be a stripper by now!' I exploded.

'Daniel, don't speak about your mother like that!'

'I'm not speaking about Mum! I'm speaking about . . . about that . . . that other . . .' But I couldn't finish the sentence. It was Mum I was talking about in a way, but in a way it wasn't. In a way I was talking about someone entirely different – about that other woman who had taken over my mother and pranced about the house in that hideous dress.

'Daniel, you must try not to think of Mum as being two different people,' Dad said gently. 'This isn't a case of Jekyll and Hyde.'

'I know that!' I mumbled stroppily. Just because I thought of Mum as being a different person when she was ill, didn't mean I didn't know that she was really just the one person as well.

'OK then,' Dad said, opening his car door. 'If you *really* already know that, then that's great.'

'What's so great about it?' I grunted, not opening mine.

'It's great because it's something *I* still find it difficult to get my head round. I find it much easier to only think about the side of your mother I feel comfortable with – the person she is when she's well – and blank out all the rest. But it's not like that, is it? It was your mother who got ill and acted that way. It was your mother who had that experience. And when she's well that experience is a part of her in the same way that all our experiences are a part of us.' He paused. 'Maybe if I'd been more able to face up to Mum's illness being a part of our lives, then I'd have been able to prepare you better and you'd have found this whole thing a lot easier to deal with.'

I stared at Dad. He was talking to me like a grown-up now, all right. I couldn't complain that he was trying to protect me too much from Mum's illness any more. And just as I was thinking that, he added firmly, 'By the way, I've decided that you're going back to school on Monday, Daniel. *Mum's* school. And when we get home, we're going to sit down together and think about how you're going to handle it if anyone says anything nasty to you about Mum.'

'But . . .' I knew from his face that there was no point in trying to argue about it. You'd think I'd be furious at having the decision suddenly taken away from me like that, but funnily enough, I wasn't. I felt something else. I felt sort of full-up inside, like my world had become pretty safe again all of a sudden. It was weird.

16

Abby called in for me on Monday morning so we could walk to school together. Dad and I had spent the previous evening going over what I was going to say if people asked me about Mum. He had even got me to pretend I was one of the other kids asking difficult questions so that he could demonstrate just how easy it was to answer them.

'My mum's been ill,' I practised saying over and over. 'She wasn't acting like her normal self for a bit, but she's getting better and she'll soon be back to normal.'

It sounded OK coming out of my mouth when Dad was looking on encouragingly. But now that I was going to have to face everybody at school for real, without Dad there, I wasn't sure that I was going to be able to get any words to come out at all.

'It'll be OK,' Abby kept saying to me as I anxiously rehearsed what I was going to say again on the way to school. 'There was an announcement in assembly about your mum being ill, so people know that's why she was behaving that way.'

'Yes, but I bet everyone's been calling her stuff anyway, haven't they? Wacko? Psycho? Mental case?'

Abby looked uncomfortable. 'Psycho mostly,' she admitted. 'But not in a really horrible way.'

I glared at her. 'How can you call someone *psycho* in a *nice* way?'

'Well, you know . . . Like in a jokey way . . . Not like they really hate her or anything . . .' She broke off.

I looked at her. I mean, what could be worse than all the kids in school calling your mum a *psycho* – and knowing that it was true? And however much I tried to remember that mental illnesses were just like any other illnesses and nothing to be ashamed of, I couldn't help wishing that Mum hadn't got one just the same.

The first person we met as we walked in through the school gate was Calum. He started to grin when he saw me. His mates were there too. 'Hey, it's Daniel! How's your mum then, Daniel? Still . . . you know . . .' He pointed to his head and made a circle with his finger to indicate *crazy*.

I was supposed to say something about Mum being ill, and leave it at that, or I was supposed to say I didn't want to talk about it and walk away calmly. But instead something else came out of my mouth. I just blurted it out.

'Oh, she's fine, thanks. All people from the planet Pluto are like her. You get used to it.'

Calum stared at me for a second like *I* was the one who had gone mad. So did Abby. His friends started to laugh, but not in a horrible way – more like they were laughing because I'd said something funny.

'That was cool,' Abby whispered as we walked away together.

'I know,' I said, trying to hide the fact that I was actually trembling. 'Just don't tell my dad, OK?'

Mum came home for the first time at the end of that week. She was just home for the weekend, but Dad reckoned it wouldn't be long before she'd be allowed home for good. When she came into my room on Saturday morning, I was sitting up in bed reading the book I had to finish by Monday for Mrs Lyle's class.

She smiled when she saw me. 'You're reading, I see. That's good.' She sat down on my bed and put her hand on my arm.

I looked at her. I was remembering being five years old and asking Dad over and over when I was going to get my mummy back. I pulled my arm away. Sometimes I didn't know if I could bear to have a mother who kept going away and then coming back again. Losing her once was bad enough, but to lose her again and not know when you were going to get her back, if at all . . . And then to have her come back and not know when you were going to lose her again . . . 'Mum, you *are* going to stay on your lithium this time, aren't you?' I asked her abruptly.

'Yes, Daniel,' she answered softly. 'This isn't going to happen again. Honestly.'

We sat silently for a moment or two. I felt bad now for having snatched my arm away like that. I reached out and touched her hand. 'You should paint your fingernails red again,' I said. 'They looked really good.'

Mum put her other hand on top of mine and squeezed it. 'Daniel, there's something I wanted to ask you. Doctor White is setting up a group for children who have a parent with a mental illness and we thought you might like to attend.'

'What sort of group?'

'A support group. Where you can talk with each other about how it feels for *you*. What do you think? They haven't done anything like this before so it'll be a bit of an experiment to start off with.'

'I don't know.' I wasn't sure I liked the sound of being part of an experiment.

'Well, think about it. You don't have to decide right now.'

'Mum, do you *have* to go back to the hospital on Monday?' I asked her.

'Yes, but Doctor White will be letting me come home for good very soon now.'

'You won't be going back to school for a while though, will you?'

'No, Daniel. Not for a while. But I will eventually. They're keeping my job open for me.'

I nodded. I would just have to deal with that when it happened. Except that maybe if I went to this group I could tell them about it and that might help.

The doorbell rang and it was the postman delivering a parcel for us from New Zealand. There were two presents inside, one for Martha and, to my surprise, one for me, and there was an envelope for Dad.

'It's Grandma's china doll!' Martha exclaimed, as she opened her present and pulled out the doll from its layers of protective packaging.

'I meant to bring that back with me,' Dad said, staring at the doll. 'In all the rush, I forgot.'

My present looked more boring. I unwrapped it and found some books inside. There was a note too: *I wanted you to have these for when you get a bit older. I was very impressed with your cocktail-making skills last year. Love from Grandma.* I showed it to Mum and Dad. It felt weird getting a note from a dead person. I looked at the books. There were three of them and they looked old. They were all cocktail recipe books.

'How lovely that she wanted you to have those, Daniel,' Mum said, smiling at me. I nodded, though I didn't think the books were all *that* lovely. Still, at least Grandma had thought about me before she died, which was kind of nice.

'What's she trying to do? Turn him into an under-age drinker?' Dad grunted. 'I think we'll have to keep these for you until you're old enough to use them, Daniel.'

'This one is a book of non-alcoholic cocktails,' Mum said, handing it to me to have a look. Sure enough, it was full of recipes for the sort of drinks I'd been making when we all went to New Zealand together last year.

'I could show Abby how to make one of these fruit ones for her mum,' I said. 'She's still in the clinic and she hasn't had any alcohol since she went in.'

'That's good,' Dad said softly. 'Let's hope she keeps it up.'

'Do you think she will, Dad?' I asked him.

He looked at me. 'Like I said, Daniel. I *hope* so.' And I realized it was another one of those times when Dad was giving me the real answer without saying the words. The real answer was that he didn't know. Nobody did. And I was just going to have to accept that.

And even though it was unfair, so was Abby.

Dad was opening his envelope now. Inside were some black-and-white photographs. His eyes started to well up as he looked at them. 'I've never seen these before. Pictures of my mother when she was a child.' His voice sounded weak like he'd got a frog in his throat (as Grandma liked to say if someone's voice went hoarse). 'You'd think she would have shown them to me, wouldn't you? But she never did.' And then he was crying like I'd never seen him cry before, with big tears trickling down his face.

I stared at him, horrified. In amongst all the other things that had been happening, I'd totally forgotten that Dad had just lost one of the most important people in his life – his mother. Just like I had nearly lost mine.

Mum quickly took over. She sent Martha and me to make him a cup of tea and by the time we brought it back to him, Dad had stopped crying, though his eyes still looked watery and red. Mum was sitting close to him, holding his hand.

Dad looked at us more fondly than he normally did when all we had done was walk into a room. 'Thanks, kids,' he said softly as he took the tea from us.

'Is it too milky?' I asked, frowning. 'I let Martha put the milk in and she poured in half the bottle.'

'I did not!' Martha protested, glaring at me.

Dad laughed and held up his hand like he was calling for a truce. 'It's perfect.'

It was just then that Mum caught sight of one of

the photographs of Grandma as a child, which Dad had let fall on to the floor. 'Goodness,' Mum said, picking it up. 'She looks like Martha.'

'Let's see.' Martha and I leaned over her shoulder to have a look. The little girl in the picture had fair hair, just like my sister

I looked at Mum. '*Now* we know,' I said.

Mum nodded. 'Not that it really matters.'

'*What* doesn't matter?' asked Martha, lifting up her new doll and tipping it upside down to see if it was wearing any knickers.

'That you look like your grandma,' Mum said, putting her arm round my sister. 'What are you going to call her then?'

Martha thought for a moment. Then she beamed at us, as if she had just thought of something very clever. 'Elizabeth!' she announced. 'Because *that's* the ward that made Mummy better!'

I stared at her. My sister comes out with some funny things sometimes, she really does.

17

That's just about it, as far as this story goes, except to say that I did go to that children's group up at the hospital. The group lasted eight weeks, but a few of us stayed in touch afterwards and it set some of us off writing to each other. They told us in the group that writing stuff down can help you to work through your feelings about things. Sometimes we had to write things down between sessions, like ten reasons why we were angry with our parent who'd been ill or ten reasons why we still loved them. (I only did the homework if it wasn't too slushy.) Anyway, after the group finished, I found I wanted to write down some more stuff, so I decided I'd write this.

All of us in the group had a different story to tell. All of our parents got ill differently, so the things we experienced were different too. Some kids had far scarier stories to tell than mine. And some of us got our parents back again at the end of it whereas some kids didn't.

Mostly I reckoned I was one of the lucky ones.

I talked quite a lot in the group about the thing I was dreading the most – Mum starting back at school. Most people at school had been OK to me since I'd started back myself and I'd begun to make some other friends there as well as Abby. But what would they all say when I started being not just me, but the head-teacher's kid again? Correction – the *mad* head-teacher's kid.

Talking about my fears helped a bit, but nothing could prepare me for the moment when Calum approached me in the playground at morning break on Mum's first day back. I'd known this was going to happen sooner or later. Abby had gone to buy something from the tuck shop, so I was on my own, which was obviously the reason why he'd picked this time to do it.

'Is it true your mum's back?' he asked. 'Because my dad says he's not sure if he wants me to keep going to a school where the head is a *mental* case!'

His mates, who were standing right behind him as usual, all laughed.

I tried to think of a smart reply, but this time I couldn't. I was too worried myself about what it was going to be like now that Mum had started back at school again. I could feel my lip beginning to tremble. I knew I mustn't cry. Whatever else happened, I mustn't let Calum see me cry. I turned away quickly.

In the group they'd taught us that it's what you tell yourself that really helps you in difficult situations, and I reckon that's true. Because right then I told myself that maybe some of Calum's mates – the nicer ones – *wouldn't* be laughing at me if they really knew how I felt inside, or if they were less scared of being picked on themselves if they didn't side with Calum. That helped a bit.

I also reminded myself of something that Dad is always saying – that in some situations you just have to be brave. Which reminded me of something else I'd heard about in the group – *ignore muscles*. I'd thought our group leader was daft when she'd first mentioned them. I'd laughed and said that there was no such thing. But then one of the other kids had pointed out that you had to be pretty strong to ignore some of the things that other kids said to you, and everyone had agreed. So we'd all said we'd have a go at ignoring people when they were horrible to us to see if that made our ignore muscles any stronger.

I decided to try mine out now. I walked away from Calum and all his jeering mates with my head held high, pretending I was Superman, who didn't have any time to waste listening to stupid bullies like them. That helped a bit more.

That's when I spotted Mum. She was crossing the playground on her way back from the teachers' car park, carrying a bundle of papers which I guess she'd just been to fetch from her car. She'd had her hair cut yesterday and it really suited her. Her tummy still stuck out, but I didn't care. Suddenly I knew that there was something else I could do to show Calum that I wasn't going to let him push me around.

'HI, MUM!' I called out loudly.

Out of the corner of my eye I could see Calum's jaw dropping open like he was totally gobsmacked. And that helped a *lot*.